Thomas

Enjoy the book

Paul Hunt.

MASHUP CORPORATIONS

The End of Business as Usual

Andy Mulholland

Chris S. Thomas

Paul Kurchina

with Dan Woods

Evolved Technologist Press
New York, NY

Mashup Corporations: The End of Business as Usual
A Chronicle of Service-Oriented Business Transformation
Andy Mulholland, Chris S. Thomas, Paul Kurchina with Dan Woods

Published by Evolved Technologist Press, an imprint of Evolved Media
Network, 242 West 30th Street, Suite 801, New York, New York 10001

This book may be purchased for educational, business, or sales promo-
tional use. For more information contact:
Evolved Technologist Press
(646) 827-2196
info@EvolvedTechnologist.com
www.EvolvedTechnologist.com

Editor/Analyst: Dan Woods
Writers: Dan Woods, Greg Lindsay
Production/Copy Editor: Deb Gabriel
Cover and interior design: 1106 Design
Illustrator: Tory Moore

First Edition: September 2006

ISBN: 978-0-9789218-0-4; 0-9789218-0-1

Dedication

To my colleagues without whose collective help in lively debates
I could not have written this book, to Sharron Mora without
whose organizational skills very little would have happened, to
my wife Gwen without whose patience with my never ending
fascination with technology nothing would have happened,
plus countless friends and colleagues throughout the industry
who quite simply make it possible for it all to happen.

~ Andy Mulholland

Thanks to my wife, Andrea and the inspiration
of our children Shen and Jaime.

~ Chris S. Thomas

Thanks to my wife Erin and my sons Braeden and Tyler for
their ongoing tremendous support and dedication.

~ Paul Kurchina

Table of Contents

Foreword

When I first read Mashup Corporations: The End of Business as Usual, I instantly recognized myself in one of the story's main characters: Josh Lovecraft. As chief editor for some of Ziff-Davis' computer magazines in the mid-90's, I saw the Web bubbling up around me. I had an idea it would wreak havoc on the media world that paid my bills. But even so, print magazines are what ruled the roost.

Print magazines are tied to an incredibly rigid and expensive business process that involves the almighty deadline. If any one part of that process gets disrupted, even by a new promising idea, heads roll. I didn't want mine to be one of them.

Those magazines were on the Web at the time. But the online versions didn't live up to their potential. I couldn't envision risking print's sacred process to bring them up to snuff. Faced with the most disruptive force the IT businesses has seen since the PC, Lovecraft—CIO at the fictional Vorpal, Inc.—could not be a better caricature of my own career. Like me with the Web, he postures to protect his functional yet monolithic IT portfolio from disruption by a service-oriented approach that could actually produce more business opportunity for Vorpal by the way it empowers customers, suppliers, and employees to not only innovate, but to ultimately play a role in transforming Vorpal's business.

I was finally coerced by my boss Dan Farber into embracing the Web. Later, I repeated the same cycle when I first resisted blogging but eventually buckled. Had I not succumbed to those coercions, I might not have survived the media business. I've since learned not just to embrace change, but also to be a change agent. It's a personal philosophy that led to the founding of Mashup Camp (*www.mashupcamp.com*) within days of discovering the role that mashups will play in transforming businesses the way they transformed Vorpal's. After much arm-twisting by Vorpal CEO Jane Moneymaker, Lovecraft eventually embraces service-oriented architectures and the mashups they enable and Vorpal heads down a path that all businesses including yours must eventually follow: a path that this quick-read which introduces the idea of "Shadow IT" is brilliantly prescriptive for.

Whether you're a CxO, a mid-level manager, or someone on the front lines for your company, you need to recognize the Josh Lovecraft in you, and be prepared not just to embrace change, but to lead it. That's because, most of us don't have the luxury of a Dan Farber or a Jane Moneymaker to make us see the light. It's really up to you (or your competitor, if you get my drift).

David Berlind
Executive Editor
ZDNet
Co-Founder, Mashup Camp

Preface

This book is built from literally hundreds of engagements with business and technology executives. The book's goal is simple: to unlock the business and revenue potential of Service-Oriented Architecture (SOA) for your companies. If this book succeeds, SOA will not be seen as a technology project, but rather as an exercise in business transformation.

The educational phase of SOA is over. Now that an understanding of the technology of SOA is spreading, many executives in business, IT, and even at technology vendors are wondering: "What is this all about anyway? I can see the technical advantages, but why should I care? How will SOA mean more money for our companies?" This book addresses those questions. It is aimed at explaining the business value of SOA and of emerging, complimentary Web 2.0 technologies such as wikis, mashups, and such. A mashup corporation is one that knows how to make the most of this new potential.

The path from this book's moment of inspiration to publication is true to the central message of business transformation. Paul Kurchina, a long-time ERP customer who now runs KurMeta, an IT ecosystem development practice, discussed some initial ideas for a book with two of his colleagues, Andy Mulholland, Global CTO of Capgemini, and Chris S. Thomas, Chief Strategist at Intel Corporation. They realized that most of the attention being lavished on SOA focused on the mechanisms and technology rather than the potential to create value.

After some initial analysis, Paul, Andy, and Chris determined that for many people SOA was a solution in search of a problem. Yes, people could see the flexibility of SOA and could understand how modeling would improve development. But the step-by-step journey from those qualities of SOA to competitive advantage, remained a mystery.

This team then did what the book recommends: open the process to innovation from all sides. The process of writing a book that is normally centralized in one person's mind was now distributed across a team of innovators, each of whom brought their own knowledge and expertise. Instead of services enabling this distribution of innovation, as is the case in the story of the book, Dan Woods's Communication by Design methodology opened up the writing process. Andy, Chris and Paul's experience engaging enterprise architecture at firms around the world and their vast ecosystem of experts at vendors and large IT departments provided a real world context to expand and crystallize the message. Dan and his team of writers, editors, and designers helped craft that message into an engaging story of Vorpal, Inc. a fictional company grappling with SOA.

> **—Andy Mulholland, Chris S. Thomas, Paul Kurchina, and Dan Woods**

Acknowledgements

We want to acknowledge Shai Agassi from SAP for his thoughts and vision on Enterprise SOA; colleagues at Intel, George Moakley, Gary Haycox, Frank Welch, Alan Boucher and C. V. Vick for the years of innovative ideas; and Cindy Lu, Pam Payne and T. K. Tien for driving us to completion. Special thanks go to Jenny Clarke of Capgemini whose tremendous energy helped make this book come to life.

We also acknowledge all the professional relationships that have made this book possible, as well as the staff at Evolved Media Network for their creative and professional efforts.

Andy, Chris, Paul

Introduction

Service-Oriented Architecture (SOA) is a new structure and a set of mechanisms for organizing and isolating application functionality, built on a flexible and reusable foundation of services. But services are not drivers of business change in and of themselves. The transformations promised by SOA will never take place unless a new culture and innovative business models take shape around it. SOA will gradually expand the scope of what Information Technology (IT) can make possible, but only if leaders possess the imagination to make use of it.

Unlike most discussions of SOA that focus on its mechanisms—services, modeling, patterns, messaging, events—this book explains the shape and value of a service-enabled business and how you can lead your company through the necessary cultural transformation. You will find quite a bit in this book about mashups because they demonstrate the power of utilizing SOA capabilities. But mashups are the thin end of a larger wedge of change that SOA will bring about, while SOA represents a new era in computing evolution.

In simplest terms, SOA expands the reach of the enterprise *by allowing services to define and transform relationships.* This book will examine the five kinds of relationships upon which SOA will make the most impact:

- The relationships between a company and customer-focused innovators inside and outside the company. *How can you harness the ideas and energy of outsiders eager to help?*

- The relationships between a company and its customers. *How can you bring your customers closer to your core business processes?*

- The relationships between a company and its suppliers. *How can you strengthen the connection between yourself and your suppliers? How can you create a win-win relationship instead of an adversarial one?*

- The relationships between the IT department and the larger company. *How can IT support employee initiatives instead of stifling them? How can innovation break new ground while protecting critical data?*
- The relationships amongst the IT professionals within a company. *How can you best structure your IT resources to reflect the needs and new capabilities of SOA? How can SOA help IT balance demands (e.g. security and ease-of-use)?*

The culture that meshes best with SOA is one of empowerment and flexibility. For SOA to achieve its potential, many assumptions that have ruled business and IT must be abandoned. New rules will govern the creation of an SOA business culture, a culture that is focused on putting as much power as possible in the hands of those closest to the customer in order to create and discover new markets and to unlock value that had never previously been accessible.

It's a culture of change and experimentation, and for IT to keep up, some reorganization will be necessary. Before that happens, however, forces that are currently driving deep structural changes within companies must be acknowledged and harnessed. A partial list of those challenges follows.

ICT versus IT

A new term: Information and Communications Technology (ICT) is rapidly being adopted to refer to a larger world of possibilities and techniques that have developed since the term Information Technology (IT) was born. Here and there, where we are speaking about the future and technology, we use ICT. Primarily, we will stick with the term IT in this book referring to the IT Department itself or because for the most part we are referring to the commonly held understanding of IT, which is the application of technology in an enterprise or large organization.

"Shadow IT" & The IT Generation Gap

In the history of enterprise computing, up until this moment, IT was mostly a world unto itself, whether centralized or decentralized. The willful isolation of IT into a narrow focus on recording transactions shaped several generations' attitudes toward the role of IT within the larger context of the organization. For older executives (defined for our purposes as 45 years old and older), the traditional mode of dealing with IT involved creating requirements and then asking IT to do what needed to be done.

But in the last decade, since the advent of the Internet era, a generational split has occurred. Employees under the age of 35 (and including many who are older) entered the workplace and took for granted plentiful bandwidth, desktop productivity tools, open source software, and a wealth of networks, including social networking, peer-to-peer technologies, and other beneficiaries of Metcalfe's Law. The members of this generation seized the tools of IT production for themselves as they configured their email, cell phones, instant messaging, wikis, and blogs to help them transact business. This do-it-yourself capability has become known as Shadow IT. To maximize the impact and breadth of use of services, Shadow IT must be encouraged, supported, and officially recognized as a critical component of day-to-day operations.

 *For SOA to work, Shadow IT must be acknowledged and supported.*

The Architectural Shift Toward Mashups and Composites

It's no longer enough to simply be on the Web. The browser window is increasingly competitive real estate, and relying on advertising-infused HTML invites uncontrollable interruptions. Head to a travel web site, for example, and the first thing you're likely to notice are popup ads for the site's competitors. Such is the dark side of the Web's ongoing shift to ad-supported models.

But the pioneering efforts of independent developers in tandem with services provided by companies like Google, Amazon.com, and many others, have enabled the assembly of simple composite applications commonly called "mashups" to appear on the scene.

Mashups may run inside browsers or in new, richer environments called composite applications. They aren't based exclusively on HTML delivered by a server. Instead, mashups use services typically delivered in XML from many different sites to knit together a useful experience for the customer. Perhaps the best-known mashups marry the basic functionality of Google or Yahoo!® Maps with specialized data sets to create customized, searchable maps.

This mashup environment is self-contained and controlled. And its ease of use heralds the next generation of flexibly recombined services.

 For SOA to work, services to support mashup/composite applications must be made available.

User-driven Innovation

Mashups aren't invented during the IT department's annual offsite meetings, except for the rare exception in which an IT organization is promoting the reuse of commonly used corporate services. Instead, they spring from the minds of entrepreneurial virtuosos who are continually sifting through the services they discover on the Internet and imagining the emergent possibilities. Companies that "get" SOA do everything in their power to turn their value-creating processes into services and then place them in the hands of their most innovative thinkers whose efforts become the company's bridge to new customers. To the outside world, the company becomes increasingly defined by the services it offers others to use as a springboard for innovation and creating new kinds of business relationships.

 For SOA to work, companies must remove barriers to innovation and put tools in the hands of innovators.

Transformed Business Models

Providing services to innovators, inside the company and out, profoundly changes the way it appears to customers, partners and competitors. Some of these new business processes create markets where none existed before; others change the role the company plays within the value chain. Most of these processes feel completely unnatural at first and arrive with a complete checklist of objections and excuses explaining why they will never work. Lightweight, reusable services offer the perfect building blocks for inexpensive experiments that may fail, as expected, or may create a massive opportunity.

 For SOA to work, new and imperfect business models must be implemented so they can be debugged and perfected.

Incremental, Agile Development

Applications based on services frequently use better, more user-friendly development tools that expand the pool of potential developers far beyond the boundaries of the IT department. Ideas for new solutions will arrive in the form of half-baked applications created by lay users who start down a path toward a solution, but lack the expertise to finish it. To exploit the full potential of SOA, the development lifecycle must accept partial solutions from wherever they originate and nudge them toward completion so that their potential can be fully measured. Agile development methods are suspicious of requirements gathered in a vacuum and promote an incremental approach in which applications are built, deployed, and then improved in a succession of rapid steps. The best solutions will ultimately emerge from these small steps forward, with the final step representing the sum total of accumulated experience.

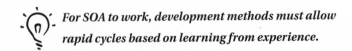 *For SOA to work, development methods must allow rapid cycles based on learning from experience.*

Governance, Security, and Operational Stability

Exposing services to the outside world inevitably places power in the hands of outsiders who are directed by their own self-interest. What are those outsiders allowed to do? How much power do they need to innovate? How can abuse be discouraged? And how can the services be created to embed rules for governance, security, and operational stability? Policies governing all of these issues and more must be created in parallel with technical efforts to build an SOA, and in many cases, will be built into the services themselves.

 For SOA to work, governance, security, and operational stability must be designed into services.

We will return to all of these topics and more as our explanation continues, but now, we must turn our attention to the real world, and to the example of Vorpal Inc., a fictional company that will undergo a transformation sparked by forces that are affecting virtually every enterprise.

Chapter 1

Why Can't We?

No amount of Information Technology (IT) spending can compel a company to change its business culture. Only individuals willing to lead in new directions can do that. This change happens in lurches, when opposition to new ideas crumbles in the face of demonstrated success.

Applying new IT capabilities is becoming a central enabler of radical organizational transformation. The playing field for this change includes the web of relationships between companies and customers, individuals and IT, and innovators on the fringe struggling to engage with likeminded peers on the outside who are separated by myriad of corporate firewalls and outdated business models. Even the technology jargon is evolving again, with SOA, XML, blogs, wikis, mashups, etc. This generation of terms is about engaging rapidly, collaboratively, and globally, frequently at a much more granular level than ever before.

Evolving to a Service-Oriented Architecture (SOA) can remove technological barriers to business process transformation. These changes bring up age-old business questions. How does one best resolve the tension between process—the slow, expensive, and occasionally quite painful march toward optimization—and achieving results, even if the path is potentially messy and ad hoc?

It is impossible to tell the story of how you can use SOA to change your business via a white paper or slide deck. As you will see, the impact of implementing SOA or engaging technology trends ultimately has less to do with the underlying technologies or a silver bullet set of business processes than it does with real and lasting cultural change. To tell the true story of SOA it's necessary to tell the story of that change and of the individuals grappling with the complications that ensue.

As we enter the world of our very fictional case study, Vorpal Inc., we enter an environment that could be repeated in nearly any industry. The challenges facing its executive team (CEO, CFO, CTO, CIO, and Line of Business (LOB) owners) certainly sound familiar. What are the best ways to find new market opportunities, strengthen the bonds with existing customers, empower employees, and seek out new suppliers, all while safeguarding the integrity of the business, its operations, and its brand?

■ The Tale of Vorpal

Our story begins in the offices of Vorpal, an appliance maker that manufactures an assortment of cooking devices, including a popcorn maker that will shortly become the center of attention. Vorpal is merely a division of a larger, more obviously fictional conglomerate, Jabberwocky Co. Vorpal posted roughly $500 million in sales last year through retail channels, a white label business with several large retailers, and a direct-to-consumer business over the Web. The relevant parts of the organizational chart are shown in Figure 1.1.

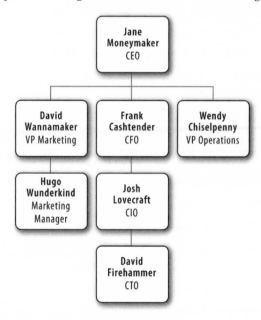

Figure 1-1: Vorpal's Organizational Chart

We open in the corner office of Vorpal CEO Jane Moneymaker, who has just finished an impromptu meeting with the young man sitting across the desk from her, a marketing manager named Hugo Wunderkind. Her door opens, and Vorpal's CIO, Josh Lovecraft, walks across the room to take a seat next to Hugo.

"Hi Josh, thanks for dropping in on short notice," Moneymaker says. "Do you know Hugo Wunderkind? He's one of our up-and-comers down in marketing, and I'm really excited about an idea he's had for our Pop-Matic line of popcorn poppers. Hugo, would you mind telling your story again for Josh's benefit?"

"Sure," Hugo says, shifting in his seat to face the CIO. "A few weeks ago, near the beginning of football season, I was sitting in our living room watching the Jets game with my family. We like to have my wife's folks over, and whoever else happens to be home, and we keep our Pop-Matic in the living room during games, so whenever anyone's feeling hungry, we just pop a new batch. During the game, my daughter Emily—who's five and discovering her passion for painting—started painting the Jets logo and Laverneus Cole's number on the side of the popper. And it just hit me—we're not the only ones who like to pop popcorn during sporting events, so why shouldn't we, Vorpal, offer Pop-Matics outfitted in real team colors? A green one with a white Jets logo in my family's case, then one for every NFL, college football, and even high school team—and that's just one sport! I thought it was a terrific idea, so I started posting about Emily's painting on my blog…"

"Wait," Lovecraft says, "you posted this internally?"

"No. I have my own Jets blog, BroadwayHugo.com, where I posted some photos of the Pop-Matic, and where I also mused that wouldn't it be cool if you could do this for every NFL team? A couple of fellow Jets fans left comments to the effect that the Pop-Matic looked great, and I found some trackbacks to other football team blogs where they wish they had the same thing for their teams—and a few guys even posted their own photos of customized poppers and other stuff—grills, …"

"That's very cool," Moneymaker interrupts. "We never knew that strain of DIY (do it yourself) sentiment existed, and I doubt we'd ever hear about it otherwise."

"Anyway," Hugo continued, "it seemed like an idea with some promise, so I talked about it with my friend Will, who runs his own software shop out on the West Coast. He helped me whip up this little widget, which we posted on my site. It's kind of a combination wiki-and-Flash application. Users can upload an image they want to see printed on the side of the Pop-Matic—something like a team logo, or a player photo, or anything that's a JPEG, really—then enter their ideas and special concerns into the wiki pages, along with ordering information into some basically dummy HTML fields—you know, your address, credit card number, etc."

"That's one intense hobby," Lovecraft says.

"I know, I know. I'm a total marketing junkie," Hugo replies, simultaneously looking a little sheepish and proud. "And I'm totally fascinated by how the Web allows ideas like this one to flourish by getting instant feedback that helps you to develop them further."

"So what happened?" Moneymaker prods.

"I woke up one morning and found an actual order in my inbox. Some college student at North Carolina State wanted to put his fraternity logo on a Pop-Matic, and he really wanted to buy it—he even entered his credit card number, which was a little crazy, considering he didn't know who I am, and the site isn't remotely secure."

"And then what happened?" asks Moneymaker.

"I just ignored it—my site wasn't configured to send him a confirmation message or anything like that, so I just figured he'd forget about it. But as it turned out, he went to a national fraternity convention the next week and passed print-outs around. I know this because 10 days later I had more than 200 orders, and traffic to my site was going through the roof, and I mean really through the roof—it was artificially high."

"What do you mean?" Lovecraft asks, looking concerned.

"Well, I started getting to the bottom of this once the orders started pouring in, and it turned out that none of these guys were Jets fans or even cared about football. (They go to ACC[1] schools, after all.) These guys were scraping my site for their frat's home page, which they then passed around in the spirit of brotherhood, I guess, and now every fraternity in America thinks we're selling these. This week alone I had 500 orders, and I configured my site to automatically send emails to every single person telling them we're back-ordered indefinitely."

---

[1] Atlantic Coast Conference

"This is a real market," Moneymaker says.

"Yes, but it isn't a real product," Lovecraft counters. "It could be, though. We actually have the capability to outsource the printing now, thanks to our revised deal with Target. Because they wanted to add bull's-eyes to their house brand of the Pop-Matic, we already have a decal supplier and a rudimentary manufacturing process. At this point it wouldn't be that much more difficult to change bull's-eyes to logos or what-have-you, provided the run is long enough."

Decal Versus Transfer

In the United States, the word "decal" means some sort of sheet of paper or plastic, usually with writing or images on it, that has an adhesive backing so it can be applied to a service. Bumper stickers are examples of decals. In many parts of the world, decal is not a common word. Instead, the same things are called "transfers".

"Make it happen," the CEO says.

"Make *what* happen?" the CIO asks incredulously.

"*This.* This new business and this new channel," the CEO replies. "Turn Hugo's customization application into a real pilot to see if this is our next business. I'll notify marketing to put Hugo on special assignment as the product's marketing manager."

Lovecraft is thunderstruck. "What he's come up with is a toy, and you're telling me we're supposed to use this toy to drive sales?

Do you have any idea how difficult and unsafe it would be to link that thing to our backend systems?"

"I don't really care, Josh," she replies coolly. "I want this business. I want these orders, and I want the rest of them that are out there that we don't know about, because we've never offered anyone the capability to customize Pop-Matics before. Our regular business has far too many competitors, and we need to find new markets to grow our revenues and volumes. In fact, we don't know what kind of market there is for customized Vorpal products of all kinds. You think there aren't Red Sox fans who wouldn't order a grill or even a fridge with their team's logo on it? I'm from Boston; you should meet my father."

"That's all well and good, Jane, but let me remind you that my team is still focused on reducing our ERP costs by 10% through license consolidation. I don't have a staff available to work on transforming his nifty little Flash app into a reliable, secure, scalable application, let alone integrating it with an outsourcer, and even if I did, it would still take me 18 months."

"But he's already done it," she insists.

"But he hasn't done it in a way that's safe," Lovecraft parries. "You heard him... twice in fact! It's not even secure. The only thing he's really done is inadvertently con 500 people into exposing themselves to identity theft last week."

Moneymaker sits up high in her chair and drops what was beginning to mount into a combative tone. "Excuse us, Hugo," she says, "but I think we need to continue this discussion of your invention privately. You've done a great job, and I'm very impressed with the initiative and creativity you've exhibited. I'd like you to research the copyright issues and costs we'll incur as we start printing logos and other things on our products. We'll be in touch soon."

"Thank you very much," he says, shaking hands with both Moneymaker and Lovecraft, while attempting to avoid eye contact with the latter.

As her door closes, Moneymaker turns back to Lovecraft to resume their argument.

"Look, I'm not claiming to know how to do this, or even how to do it right. You're supposed to tell me that. But instead, you're simply tossing out reasons why we can't do it at all. That isn't constructive."

"What he has done is not what we do," Lovecraft says evenly. "We use centralized, industrial-strength applications to keep this business running—to process orders, to keep track of inventory, to analyze the hard data coming out in business intelligence. We rely on more than just word-of-mouth among sports bloggers. I'm supposed to tell you that everything we do is safe and secure. If I were to make an application like his, I would make sure that people can't upload pornographic images onto Pop-Matics for home viewing of a different sort, and I'd ensure that hackers can't endlessly clone my application the way those frat boys have cloned his in order to go phishing for credit card numbers. That's the work I see when I look at his toy, not just the opportunity you're seeing."

"But why can't we do all of that?" Moneymaker asks, exasperated. "You're still not listening to me—these customers are real. They may be naive to give us their credit card numbers today. But why does it have to take 18 months to transform something that is simple and lightweight enough that he could literally do it himself at home into a hulking application? I can only imagine how desperate they are to own a New England Patriots Pop-Matic, and I wonder why the hell we aren't selling them one. This is real revenue and real profit, and if we don't find a way to sell these to them, you know our competitors will. Why can't we roll out applications like these separately from our ERP backend? I am willing to accept a little risk in our applications the same way I'm willing to accept risk in our business every day."

"I know you remember the mess 10 years ago when the Web was new and seemingly every department was purchasing a web server and every person in this company had a home page and was scheming to set up their own e-commerce system," Lovecraft says. " I remember the same kinds of kids in marketing yammering about 'bricks and clicks,' but what I really remember is that it took years to build a stable, secure, and most of all, profitable web presence that allowed us to sell directly to consumers..."

"I know, I know," she cuts him off. "You were right about that," she concedes. "But this time I want the benefits without the mess."

She checks her watch. "I have a lunch meeting downtown. Will you escort me to the garage so we can finish this conversation?"

They leave her office and walk down the hall to the elevator bank, still arguing, although less heatedly now, about what she perceives as a disconnect between IT's priorities and the real world needs of her business, and what Lovecraft sees as a dangerously narrow view in which the inherent risks of embracing amateur technologists are overlooked in favor of what appear to be easy profits.

The elevator's descent to the parking garage is quickly brought to a jarring halt between floors. It doesn't move after that. Moneymaker presses the help button, and a staticky voice promises that there's nothing seriously wrong; they'll have it moving again in just a few moments; sorry about the inconvenience.

Moneymaker and Lovecraft look each other in the eye. "Do you know what this is?" she asks. "This is a metaphor. We're stuck together. We're stuck together until this company is overtaken by our competitors and the powers-that-be in New York replace both of us. We need to figure this out together. Look, here's what I need from you. I want to do business in new ways. I want IT to empower someone like Hugo to generate new revenue, not to just cut costs.

"I see all of these things out there—mashups that reuse content in ways no one had ever thought of before, and now they're revenue streams. Every business magazine is full of articles about these new technologies and the businesses achieving the impossible with them. Look at Google Earth and Google Maps. Someone provides Google with all of the satellite photos and maps they use on those sites and I bet they're getting paid to do it—whether it's on Google's site, or through any of the thousands of mashups that are using their stuff. Think about that—they opened themselves up to Google; Google opened itself up to the world, and on a scale they never dreamed of before. Hugo Wunderkind's customized Pop-Matics could do this for us, and I want to at least try. But I can't do it without your help."

"Look," Lovecraft says, "you need to tell me what you need from me. This isn't like anything we've done before. You've told me to cut costs and to increase efficiencies, and that's what I'm doing. The CFO tells me to address compliance and keep our systems resilient and secure. We need to reconcile that mission with everything you want me to do now, and it's going to require new resources, new policies, and a whole new set of targets."

The elevator shudders back to life, and as they part in the garage, Moneymaker and Lovecraft promise to begin that reconciliation with emails that plainly state each other's position and act as a starting point for a new relationship between her office and his.

What Business Needs from IT

Late that night, Moneymaker sends this message:

> Date: November 21, 2006, 02:34:06
> From: Jane Moneymaker (jmoneymaker@vorpalinc.com)
> To: Josh Lovecraft (jlovecraft@vorpalinc.com)
> Cc: Frank Cashtender (fcashtender@vorpalinc.com)
> Subject: memo: where do we go from here?

Josh,

I don't know exactly what's happening in the "Web 2.0"
world, at least I don't know much more than what I read in
HBR and Business 2.0. But I know it's important. I can feel
it in my gut that there are major opportunities out there,
down this path. If we can generate 500 orders a week via
an employee's hobby, for a product that doesn't exist, then
there must be thousands, hundreds of thousands, millions
of orders across this company that don't yet exist either,
because we aren't listening to the best ideas of our own
employees, partners, or customers.

I know we've rarely talked since we reorganized IT. Frank
Cashtender, the CFO to whom you report, diligently sends me
reports on your successes every quarter, but this is a different
game. This isn't about cutting costs; this is about boosting
revenue. I want to go after this business. Now you have to tell
me, what's the shortest technology path to these customers,
and to fulfilling these orders? I can't imagine that path starts
with our centralized transaction systems, nor does it need to.
Why can't we grant the Hugo Wunderkinds of the world the
resources and access needed to pursue new customers, or
even better, let these customers engage us? If it involves

more staff, new staff, an overhaul of the org chart, then we'll do that. I need you to tell me what you need from me.

I'm willing to consider new approaches to using ICT, but I'm not willing to consider not doing this. And we have to figure this out together.

jane

Breaking the Chains of Traditional IT

The next morning, the CIO sent this reply:

Date: November 21, 2006, 09:12:09
From: Josh Lovecraft (jlovecraft@vorpalinc.com)
To: Jane Moneymaker (jmoneymaker@vorpalinc.com)
Cc: Frank Cashtender (fcashtender@vorpalinc.com)
Subject: Re: memo: where do we go from here?

Jane,

My job is overseeing, safeguarding, and optimizing the central systems of this company—ERP, CRM, and all the other three-letter acronyms that are necessary for the core operations of this business. They support, track, and fulfill everything we do. As of this moment, they are more the essence of this company than you or I, and I am reasonably confident that we could be replaced with much less harm than they could be.

What you are talking about in your email is inviting a whole slew of new people into the heart of our business. I'm not just referring to IT. If you give someone the power to register orders somewhere other than our web site, then those customers you're so eager to find will be interacting with our brands in ways we can't control. The IT integration issues are only the tip of the iceberg.

I understand that you want to go after this business in a different way; that we should be more like Hugo than he should be like us. But we have to be more like him in a manner that does not harm this business through unnecessary risk-taking, or just plain sloppiness in execution.

You need to understand that doing so will change how we do business in IT. I'm responsible to Frank for keeping our business optimized and cost efficient. Embarking on this project requires more resources than I have at my disposal today. I'd need some unencumbered people and the time and money to make it happen. Otherwise, how much time do you think would elapse before he shut the skunkworks down?

To do what you're asking requires a new IT team, focused on rapid business solution prototyping, reporting directly to you, at least at this point. It also requires a new focus for the developers of our ERP and CRM systems who will need to start the evolution of their systems to ultimately intersect the new solutions being designed. I don't know what we'll need in the long run, but I do think that, in all likelihood, we will screw things up occasionally, or maybe we'll fail early and often in the beginning before improving. We're going into a new world here, and we have to figure out how we are going to do this— to open up a piece of ourselves to outsiders that will enable us to reap all of the benefits of collaboration while protecting ourselves from the possible downsides. How can we do this and still be safe?

josh

Later that week, Moneymaker and Lovecraft meet again in her office. She agrees to form a team that will pursue opportunities like Hugo Wunderkind's, and Lovecraft agrees to see it through with her.

■ Rules

The rules at the end of each chapter have little or nothing to do with specific technologies and everything to do with creating a corporate culture prepared to compete in the services-enabled era. It's unlikely that your own path to SOA will be as smooth as Vorpal's (and there will no doubt be detours), but consider these as guideposts.

Rule:
Business Imagination Drives Architecture

Pay close attention to how the Vorpal story didn't begin: with the CIO striding into his CEO's office and demanding, apropos of some vague promises about a glorious future, that she authorize service-enabling every application in sight. Instead, it began with a specific idea that sprang from the business imagination, and the theme of this book is the deployment of services for the service of these concrete ideas, rather than for the sake of too-vague-to-be-useful concepts like "flexibility."

One of the aspects of SOA that scares CIOs and other executives the most is the prospect of "mission creep"—the slow, uncontrollable growth in a project's scope until it becomes unmanageable. Complicating the issue is the fact that essentially anything and everything can be service-enabled—your web site, your ERP system, even your cell phones—and that sooner or later everything will be.

But creating and consuming services in the pursuit of an idea, especially a tactical initiative with immediate benefits, automatically focuses IT's efforts on the services needed for implementation. Hugo Wunderkind's serendipitous discovery of a new market opportunity for Vorpal is just such an idea, and the scope of the resulting IT project is defined by the immediate business needs posed by it, just as the size of the potential investment is matched by the size of the potential opportunity. That's why in the hierarchy of systems that are categorized as "stable," "flexible," and "dynamic," it's the last group—including most if not all of the systems reacting to marketing forces acting upon the business—where SOA can be implemented with maximum effectiveness.

In other words, focus SOA efforts on business innovation, rather than grope for ideas to justify adapting your IT environment to an SOA.

Rule:
Focus SOA Innovation on New Revenue

In most companies, IT is perceived as a necessary evil—the costly infrastructure that must be continually kept pruned—and SOA has been touted as the next mechanism to do so. IT rarely represents SOA as a business enabler—a font of new technologies and new ideas for pleasing customers and increasing revenues. But as Hugo's brainchild posits, SOA is capable of doing just that.

That doesn't mean IT stops being a necessary evil; it still is in the CFO's mind. But in the CEO's mind, à la Jane Moneymaker, it's anything but. In the emerging SOA environment, IT organizations assume a certain duality—it's simultaneously a cost center and a revenue creator, thus serving two masters: the CFO *and* the CEO. A radical change in the relationship of IT to the rest of the business must occur as ICT becomes part of a company's service delivery. As we've seen, CIOs will need to have heart-to-heart conversations with their respective masters to begin figuring out how this will happen.

A major shift already underway is the evolution of "edge" IT, which is entirely different from traditional or "hub" IT. In this characterization (explained in detail below), traditional IT applications such as ERP are seen as residing at the center, i.e. the hub of the business, and connected to the front lines by spokes comprised of stable business processes. On the edge of this imagined wheel are employees responding to moment-by-moment business opportunities or challenges. "Edge IT" (frequently characterized as Web 2.0) represents the organic efforts by these employees and the "uber" industry to develop creative, frequently ad hoc, tools to aid them. In the story above, Hugo is a perfect example of someone practicing edge IT, while his CIO is the walking embodiment of hub IT.

Rule:
Expect Perpetual Beta

SOA represents a new phase in how to do business, and the full possibilities (along with limitations) are not yet clear. This chapter is the beginning of our story, and it also represents the current state of the larger SOA story at most companies: no one yet knows where it will all end. The term "perpetual beta" has been batted around the developer community to stand in for the idea that solutions evolve and are continually being worked on and improved. This might give traditional project managers heartburn, but Vorpal's CEO already knows that Hugo's lead must be followed, just as her CIO is aware that he doesn't yet know how to support him. The lesson here isn't that everyone must instantaneously know their roles within the company to make SOA succeed; that's impossible. But what's critical is that everyone trusts each other enough to find a way forward, and eventually, through iterative successes, the path becomes clear.

■ Putting the Rules to Work

In this section and the ones like it that follow in each chapter, issues that arise when the rules are applied will be analyzed and discussed. Here we take a look and a new perspective on IT that distinguishes between traditional transaction-focused applications and a new generation that has interaction as its goal.

Hubs and Edges: The Two Domains of IT

The traditional idea of how IT functions within organizations—as a unit separate from the front lines of the business, tending to core infrastructure and devoted to continually slashing its cost—breaks down within SOA. Traditional IT works with monolithic applications (ERP, CRM, and the like) that receive and process transactions and other forms of data within a closed, proprietary, highly secure environment. This picture isn't necessarily false in SOA, but it's no longer the whole picture. Because, in addition to these core processes, there are an increasing number of individuals on the front lines exploiting the opportunities for collaboration and cross-pollination created by blogging, wikis, Flash, and so on. These ad hoc activities aren't IT in the traditional sense, where IT is focused solely on structured processes in the core of the organization, the innovators of these activities are seeking to optimize individual transactions and their own small pieces of the business on the fly. But their efforts, which have been dubbed "shadow IT" by some, represent an important evolution in IT—one that co-exists with the traditional model, rather than competes with or replaces it. There are already examples of structured, traditional hub IT applications which have migrated to the edges, such as e-commerce engines and SCM applications.

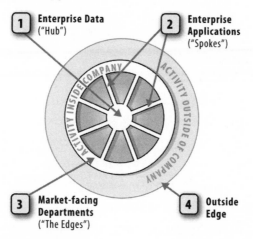

Figure 1-2: IT Hubs and Edges

The best analogy and image to describe these divergent strains of IT is that of a wagon wheel, with traditional IT at the center—the "hub"—the front lines of the business on the rim of the wheel—the "edges"—and transactional data flowing back to the hub via "spokes," as illustrated in Figure 1-2. Why the shape of a wheel? Because it represents the 360-degree relationships made possible by edge IT, as opposed to the traditional IT architecture in which suppliers are connected to the "back" of the enterprise with customers facing the "front."

In SOA, the activities within the hub continue more or less as they always have, whether service-enabled or not. It's on the edges where SOA flourishes, as the edges also represent the literal edge of the company in the form of the firewall, where standardized, service-enabled messages pass back and forth through the membrane. It's here where a generation of young employees (from 35 years old on down) have mastered both the hardware (PCs, cell phones, wireless devices, etc.) and software (blogging, wikis, etc.) that drive the emerging culture of collaboration and social computing that has been called a hallmark of "Web 2.0."

It's here on the edges where services can make the greatest impact as the links between the functionality carried from applications residing in the hub to innovators at the edges. The "inside edge" is where corporate innovators are using services and other tools to enhance their relationships with suppliers, partners, and customers, while the "outside edge" actually lies on the far side of the firewall. The innovators there are customers, suppliers, benign hackers, and other interested third parties with enough affection and attachment to the company to willingly give their time and energy to developing new uses for the services provided to them (à la the fraternity brothers who have already stumbled across Hugo's application and recast it for their own purposes).

As we will see in later chapters, the implications of the hub and edge model go far beyond how best to structure IT departments, and will lead Vorpal to question and overturn what had once been central tenets of its organization.

Web Services

Web services are what make many mashups possible. Web services are standard approaches to exposing the capabilities of a company's web site or internal systems to other web sites or systems by bypassing the user interface and connecting directly to the underlying technology. In choosing to make it's database of events available for incorporation into other software and web sites, *Eventful.com* runs a web service that sits on the Internet, waiting to service requests from outfits like *Podbop.org*. After Eventful's web service responds to a request from Podbop (or any other site or software) with a set of results, Podbop take those results and incorporates them into a final result that's then presented to the end user. See the Appendix for more information on web services and service-oriented architecture

◼ Examples

Hugo Wunderkind's mashup-fueled roller coaster ride explained in the story of Vorpal is exciting and fast moving, but not at all unrealistic. Podbop, *www.podbop.org,* is just one of many examples of mashups that have arrived on the scene and taken hold quickly.

Podbop

Podbop is a poignant example of how the wealth of web services (see box), delivering content of all sorts, and the power of open source development tools has changed the clockspeed for product development. In less than 5 months of part-time work, Podbop went from an idea to an implemented product that gained international attention.

Podbop launched its mashup relating MP3 music recordings to upcoming events just before the February 2006 Mashup Camp Unconference. It won the competition for best mashup, had a flurry of press coverage including mentions by news organizations such as Wired, Forbes, Newsweek and the BBC. As of August 2006, the site is supported by Google AdSense revenue, and the developers are considering expanding the range of business models.

While he was a student at the University of Florida, Taylor McKnight got in the habit of looking up MP3s for the bands that were coming to town. Taylor loves music and was frequently disappointed to find that he missed excellent shows because he saw a listing but never found an MP3 to hear what the band sounded like. When a new online service called Eventful.com was launched helping users list and find upcoming events, Taylor realized that by adding MP3s to the Eventful event listings database, his informal habit could be turned into a product.

In October 2005, Taylor, who would graduate in May 2006 with a degree in marketing, discussed his idea with Daniel Westermann-Clark, who graduated in May 2004 with a degree in computer engineering. The two became acquainted through their full-time jobs at the University of Florida Web Administration office, where they worked together on a variety of web sites and services for the campus community.

Daniel, an expert programmer in the Perl programming language, used the Perl-based Catalyst framework for web site development along with the Eventful web services to achieve Taylor's vision. Within two weeks the two had a working version of the site, which mashes the event listings with MP3s that are uploaded by Podbop community members around the world. The community involvement is a key part of Podbop because members gather MP3s distributed all over the Internet and upload them to a central location. Podbop's architecture is shown in Figure 1-3:

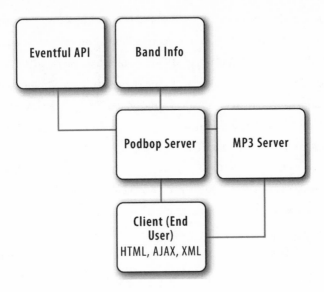

Figure 1-3: Podbop Architecture

The Podbop site averages more than 50,000 page views a month and more than 20,000 unique visitors. Seventy five different record labels have their full catalog of recordings on the site, and many more labels have also contributed parts of their catalogs. Independent artists have started using the site as a way to build an audience. There are just short of 5,000 MP3s on Podbop now, a number that is constantly growing. New features added since launch include special pages to cover the artists at festivals and a podcast for each city on the site.

Chapter *2*

Company and Innovators

In the few weeks that have passed since the first meeting of Jane Moneymaker, Josh Lovecraft, and Hugo Wunderkind, a new feeling is palpable in Vorpal's offices. Moneymaker is excited; she has stumbled upon a potentially huge revenue stream that she never knew existed. But she's nervous, too. She knows that Lovecraft, her CIO, is right to have his reservations. The company simply can't throw open their doors to well-meaning hackers and other passionate customers regardless of consequences. However, she is eager enough to open the door halfway to bring these outside innovators into the fold.

Lovecraft is uncomfortable; the idea of employing ad hoc services created by consumers themselves has, needless to say, come from outside of his department. And what's making him more nervous is the fact that the code powering those services exists outside of his domain entirely.

Hugo Wunderkind, for his part, is utterly thrilled that his idea—his hobby, really—has captured the imagination of the CEO and is becoming a real revenue stream for Vorpal. His mind is racing, as each day seems to bring more opportunities to expand the reach of the phenomenon he's nurtured.

We now pick up the story before a teleconference that Hugo has arranged with the college students who first discovered his site, and who are the ones responsible for making it a sensation.

Outsider Innovators

At precisely 10 A.M. on Wednesday morning, Josh Lovecraft and Jane Moneymaker appear in the doorway of the Maize conference room, in which Hugo Wunderkind and the inner circle of his marketing team are already seated, listening to a laconic drawl emanating from a speaker in the middle of the table.

"...it's our pleasure. But seriously, when are y'all going to send us our poppers?" the voice says. "I understand that they aren't exactly real right now, but can't you send us some prototypes? We've got an away game at Maryland next weekend, and we could really use one."

"Uh, I don't know about that," Hugo says hesitantly, waving them in. "The whole point of this call is to figure that out, which is why I'd like to introduce the three of you to my bosses—Jane

Moneymaker and Josh Lovecraft. Josh runs the technology arm here at Vorpal, and Jane runs the company, so they have the biggest say in when we can send you your Pop-Matics.

"They've joined us here on the call, and I'd like to introduce Josh in particular to the three of you. Josh, would you please say hello to Alex Vachon, Greg Garringer, and Dana Veis? They're the president, vice president and secretary, respectively, of the Delta Rho Upsilon North Carolina State University Chapter."

"Hi guys," Moneymaker says to the phone. "You know, I have to confess that it kills me a little bit to hear that a couple of guys from NC State came up with this first." The phone is deadly silent. "I'm a Tarheel, you see," and at that, a staticky squeal of laughter fills the room. "A State alum would have had this figured out by now," one of them says.

"But seriously, guys," Moneymaker continues, "we're really excited by what you've done with Hugo's software, and I'd like you to explain exactly how you did it, because we really feel this is a huge opportunity for us, and we'd really like to help you and others like you."

"Well, we all grew up eating popcorn from Vorpal poppers," the voice identified as Alex says. "Greg here is from New Jersey, and he read Hugo's Jets blog and saw the Pop-Matic. We love the Pop-Matic, and we were really excited to discover what we thought was a way to order poppers with our Delta Rho Upsilon letters for ourselves, and Wolfpack poppers for our fathers. We're still hoping we can—with Christmas coming, we were excited about buying some as gifts, too... But in any case, Greg was the one who found the blog, which wasn't very hard—it's one of the top hits for the Jets on Google now, and when we went back later, we found it was the top hit for 'Pop-Matic' as well..."

Moneymaker shoots Hugo a look across the conference table and mouths "Really?" Hugo nods emphatically.

"...We loved Hugo's application, and when we emailed him to tell him that, he didn't write back, at least not at first. We all bought poppers, or at least we thought we did. Then a week later, I was at the national Delta Rho Upsilon convention telling brothers in other chapters that they could order custom Delta Rho Upsilon Pop-Matics just as easily as they could order up t-shirts from Café Press. They wanted to know where, and we decided 'we' being me, Dana, and Greg that we shouldn't be buying them from a Jets blog. So Dana—here, Dana, you tell the story..."

"I'm in charge of the national Delta Rho Upsilon home page," Dana says, picking up the thread, "so I decided to clone Hugo's application and put it on our site. The orders would still be processed by Vorpal (we thought), but that way it seemed like it was a semi-official Delta Rho Upsilon initiative. I'm studying finance, but I knew enough to scrape the output of Hugo's forms and copy his Flash app with a little tweaking. I just changed the logo and tossed it up on our site, and it turned out to be really popular—even our brothers studying abroad in London this semester wanted one for watching Manchester United games. Hugo eventually started writing back to us when hundreds of orders started pouring in. We've seen other fraternities clone their own copies as well. It's even been highlighted as a good example of a commercial mashup on the wiki of some event called MashupCamp. But, um, we still don't have a popcorn popper here in the house."

"We want you to have a Delta Rho Upsilon Pop-Matic," Moneymaker says, "and we want everyone who wants a custom Pop-Matic to be able to buy one. That's what this call is about. In the meantime, I am going to immediately send you a Pop-Matic from my office. Teddy," she says to her assistant, who has been hovering in the doorway the entire time, "can you make sure we get 15 poppers to Delta Rho Upsilon tomorrow? Thanks."

Lovecraft holds up a hand to signal that he'd like to begin his interrogation now. "All right, I'd like to hear some of the technical details of how you created the application on your site," he says. "So, you're scraping Hugo's site and returning the results. How? Because when I tried, it tended to break a little bit. I kept getting runtime errors every fourth or fifth try when I was testing it on a vanilla Typepad account I used as my testbed."

"We used a simple PHP script, and then we hard-coded the screen size to return the image. But yeah, it does tend to break," Dana says, "especially if the image is too big—both in terms of file size or actual print size. I wanted to do this cool wraparound Delta Rho Upsilon logo using only text, and I just about destroyed the site as a result. But most of the time it works."

"So if he was to change the screen at all on his blog, the whole thing would break…" Lovecraft interrupts.

"Yeah, that's true," Dana concedes. "If he changes the screen, we'll have to figure it out and change it ourselves to keep up. But we have a test script in place to make sure it runs properly—to make sure our brothers weren't receiving error messages left and right or accidentally ordering five or six poppers because the page didn't refresh after they clicked 'submit.'

"But look, I know that scraping isn't the right way to do this," he adds, "but I whipped this up just before writing a term paper about three hours before it was due. So it's kind of intentionally crappy. A couple of the CompSci majors in the house saw what I did and started laughing because it was too crappy in their eyes. But they said that if Vorpal gave them some XML API's or web services to play with, they could whip up a totally reliable application for our site independently of Hugo's thing. They have the tools and they know what they're doing…." He trails off.

"Where's the site hosted?" Lovecraft asks.

"On one of GoDaddy.com's servers somewhere," Dana replies. "We just have a standard-issue hosting package."

"How much traffic does the site get?"

"Not much, and we can't handle a lot either, which is why I've just been passing my little hack along to other fraternities who ask for it, rather than having them pound our site or Hugo's. Let them pay for their own bandwidth, you know?"

"Oh, I know," says Lovecraft. "Thanks guys, I don't have any further questions."

"Hey guys," Hugo says, beginning to wrap up the call. "This has been great; I really appreciate your taking the time to talk to us, and let us know when your Pop-Matics arrive. If we think of anything else, we'll drop you all emails."

"Anything we can do to help show a Tarheel the light is our pleasure," Alex says. "Put it down to North Carolina courtesy." The NC State students say their goodbyes and drop off the call. After some throat clearing by Hugo, Lovecraft takes control of the floor.

"Look," he says, "you're talking about a couple of college kids who aren't especially great hackers. They figured out how to reverse-engineer your application, but the result is just terrible, seen from a performance aspect. It breaks; you can never be sure if your order has been received or not... or how many orders have been received; and there's absolutely no quality control or checks on the images being submitted. You could use this as a tool for print porn, hate speech, copyright and trademark infringement, and so on. If we did something like this and actually released it in its current state, the same bloggers who are touting this idea now would come after us with the blogging equivalent of pitchforks and torches. And then, Jane, you'd fire me for having approved it."

"That may be true, Josh," Moneymaker says softly at the far end of the table, "but they received 500 orders last week..."

"And they've received another thousand since then," Hugo chimes in. Moneymaker's eyebrows arch reflexively.

"But this is amateur hour IT..." Lovecraft begins.

"They aren't amateur hour orders," she says. "They're real ones. And I sent instructions this morning to our Malaysian plant to fulfill them. We'll have to do it with brute force for now—we'll have Emblazon print up decals (although, for some reason, they call them 'transfers' on their site)—and apply them by hand until we can figure out how to automate the process.

"Josh, our business isn't winning IT awards; our business is offering products our customers want to buy and then fulfilling their orders. So far, we've gotten it half right, but these college kids came up with the other half. Why can't your team help them out? What about this web services thing they mentioned?"

"Well...we could give them API's to order without actually hard wiring directly to our transaction systems. We could validate the orders and submit the real ones via a batch process later. Hiding our moving parts behind service calls could work, and providing an official Flash application from Vorpal that they can download and embed on their sites would make me feel a lot safer."

"So what's stopping you?"

Empowering the Outside Edge

Over the next hour, the CEO, CIO, Hugo and the new product team hammer out a plan of action for building open, reusable services to replace Hugo's, and for responsibly deploying them. Their checklist looks something like this:

1. Create a stable, reliable, high-performance Flash application and offer it as a free download to interested parties for personalization and integration into their own solutions.

2. Develop services that enable outside developers, but also limit exposure to core business systems by:

    A) Creating a set of web services capable of processing orders coming from the Flash application, and preparing them for manual validation before entering batches of orders into Vorpal's backend systems. Fully automating this process will be addressed after a profitable business model is proven and cost savings over the manual workload justify the effort.

    B) Exploring possibilities for using the same web services with known business partners' systems without the Flash application.

3. Establish a plan for educating amateur developers in the nuances of intellectual property law, appropriate usage and good taste. Then engage the legal department to establish an opt-in licensing model that explicitly states intended usages and that anyone caught violating the agreement for the Flash application (which would include clauses banning pornography, hate speech, etc.) would be disconnected from the system and subject to prosecution.

4. Develop sales and marketing collateral and:

   A) Engage immediate opportunities (those without copyright, trademark or licensing complications); and

   B) Begin approaching professional sports leagues (the NFL) and college teams (the NCAA) about licensing their members' logos, etc. for use on Pop-Matic poppers. Investigate royalty fees, etc. and arrive at an official list of acceptable logos; and

   C) Identify international opportunities.

■ Rules

One of the most frequent (and frequently wrong) assumptions is that service-enablement is only an internal IT matter, and that the best uses of SOA are service-enabling already existing applications. As this chapter and these rules demonstrate, there's untapped value in using an SOA to extend IT to the edges of your organization and beyond—even to your customers themselves—if there's an opportunity to involve them in activities that create value for both sides (like designing your next products).

Rule:
Combining Services Compounds Benefits

Collaborating and working with your ecosystem of fellow travelers is a new corporate competence. As the young men of Delta Rho Upsilon prove, when it comes to discovering new market opportunities and galvanizing product development, the more brains the better. Combining Vorpal's application with their fraternity services instantly created a new business channel. Your company may know its existing customers well, but how can it possibly know all of its potential customers? Exposing a service offers opportunities to outsiders—including your customers—to impact and extend your business and theirs. They can potentially add their own services that create new revenue streams with little work on your own part—provided you offer them the motivation to do so. It's the difference between trying to control the environment outside your business versus inspiring and enabling them.

The flip side to this dynamic is that these outsiders want what they want, in terms of access and functionality, and not necessarily what you'd prefer to give them. Using services effectively, it's possible to define the limits and scope of the functionality at their disposal with less active supervision on your part.

Rule:
Valuable Services Cross Firewalls

Closed companies are limited to their own resources, competencies and views. One of IT's first instincts when grappling with SOA is to create every service behind the firewall, because it's easier and safer. The idea of granting outsiders not just a user interface, but an actual programming interface terrifies them. Now the barbarians outside the gates have real power! And who knows what malevolent hackers lurk in the shadows, just waiting for your WSDL (Web Service Definition Language) to come their way.

But if your company doesn't use services to extend your business beyond the firewall, it's missing the revenue opportunities associated with services. Inside the firewall, what chance do you have of creating a truly new business architecture with SOA, rather than simply moving the furniture around? Services deployed internally can be valuable for reducing the costs of IT, but services created for external consumption feed users on the edges, where the new business opportunities lie. Take informed risks and open up processes by providing APIs to the world that facilitate safe and controlled access across your firewalls.

Rule:
Empower the Edge

Edge IT is actually two edges: the inside edge, comprised of Hugo and his ilk—the corporate innovators often struggling for legitimacy within the organization—and the outside edge, made up of external programmers, hackers, and enlightened customers who are ready and eager to work in the marketplace, in exchange for recognition or profit.

Empowering internal innovators like Hugo means providing the incentive, permission and tools (resources) to initially succeed. Ultimately, they need a voice to make themselves and their results heard by management, and will flourish in a corporate culture that embraces turning successful Shadow IT efforts into official processes.

Those on the outside edge—like the NC State students in this chapter—need clear boundaries and a clear definition of the implications of entering a business relationship with your company by utilizing your service. While many external online policies are written to keep others out, these service agreements will encourage external engagements by creating a contract with your ecosystem partner. Establishing clear accountability aids everyone involved by providing the legal context for expected behavior, business use or revenue generated from the services.

■ Putting the Rules to Work

To put these rules to work and thereby open up your business through services, care must be taken and new relationships must be carefully managed. It can be done quickly, but it must be done safely and methodically as well.

Starting Safely

When companies first began devising web strategies more than a decade ago, most of them started quite simply. The thinking was: "let's find out what works." The first e-commerce sites and portals to appear rarely had direct links to hub systems; most companies were more than willing to manually transfer transaction data from their internet efforts to their enterprise applications. While that practice sounds unacceptably slow and complicated in hindsight, it also served to insulate early efforts from catastrophe, and, in turn, to inspire organizations to experiment freely.

It's a good idea to resurrect that attitude and those practices when beginning to work with services. Start with a simple set of well-tested services that are disconnected from any critical or delicate processes; don't worry about building slick-looking solutions on Day One.

Rather than adopt the circa-1996 attitude of "build it, and they will come," a better mantra might be "they will come and help build it." One of the defining trends of the Web 2.0 era, so far, has been the desire of independent innovators—such as entrepreneurs, open source advocates, talented amateurs, etc.—to track down and work with like-minded corporations for their mutual benefit. Think of your first set of services as an advertisement for yourself aimed at the innovators hovering out there, because they *will* find you.

Google, for example, has begun indexing executable files currently living on sites around the Web. While the primary use of this capability so far has been to hunt down malware, it's not a stretch to imagine an enthusiastic hacker using that ability to search for code strings which interest him, and which may lead him straight to your door. His or her interest—and the interest of an entire community of innovators—will ultimately aid you in securing your services and helping you chart your next step forward.

Marketing to Innovators

Once you've succeeded in attracting like-minded souls to your services, you can afford to become more selective. Who do I want to work with? What can we offer each other? And how much do they really need to know about the internal workings of our business?

You should accept as a given that most outside innovators will ultimately be indifferent to your goals; a few will no doubt be malicious (thus the need for extensive testing beforehand), and a handful, if you're lucky, will freely offer you the value-adding fruits of their imaginations.

The trick is not only attracting that handful while protecting yourself from the crowd, but also proactively identifying and recruiting them. The rise of the blogosphere and of social networking sites has made it easier than ever to discover and keep tabs on a virtual farm team of talent working on the Web today. Rather than wait for them to discover your services, you should send out feelers to innovators who share similar interests and aims. But how do you simultaneously attract them with interesting services, while protecting yourself until you can trust their intentions?

Fortunately, because services inherently operate on a need-to-know basis—which is to say that the underlying functionality is shielded behind the service interface—it's a relatively simple matter to offer only superficial descriptions of how the services you've exposed matter in the larger context of your business. You can hand out services for interested innovators to play with, but you can wait until after they've proven themselves before you draw them into your organization. At that point, it becomes a question for the legal department—How is that relationship defined? What are the incentives for both sides? Your outside innovator has essentially become an unconventional contract employee.

Fear of the Unknown

The biggest obstacle to the scenario illustrated in this chapter is the great fear of the unknown—no doubt compiled into a list of counter-examples by a nervous executive eager to dismiss the idea of working with anyone outside the company. Innovators? What about hackers, incompetents, and spies from our competitors? What if the great mass of brainpower assembled to build our next products or business processes for free decides to discover and exploit a flaw in our security instead? What if a competitor learns of our next-generation products this way?

One response is to see outside innovators in the same light as any other effort to build communities around your company and its products. Your competitors can just as easily learn about your upcoming projects at trade shows or conferences, in your online communities, and in any other public forum in which you seek feedback from a community of your partners, peers, press, and so forth. Yes, inviting outsiders to use services is potentially much scarier than those traditional outlets, because rather than simply reacting to your internal development, they've actually been invited to participate in the process of creation.

But that participation also happens to be the greatest argument in favor of services, and protecting yourself, as we've stressed above, is simply a question of securing and rigorously testing publicly available services beforehand. Once that's finished, focus instead on using services to multiply the benefits of your community by tapping directly into their creative energies, rather than using them, as you always have, as purely a feedback mechanism.

■ Examples

If you build it, they will come, is the underlying philosophy of many product development processes. In an SOA world, a new option is possible: Let them come and help build it. Companies like ESRI have shown that this is much more than epigrammatic cleverness. Putting services in the right hands creates new markets.

ESRI—Mashing Up Maps With Services

Environmental Systems Research Institute (ESRI) has been the market leader in the suddenly hot market of geographic information systems (GIS) for more than 30 years. In other words, it sells a lot of maps. And while Google Maps popularized the map mashup by opening its API to the world, ESRI was quietly rewriting many of its classic server- and desktop-based offerings as web services. Today, the company offers its customer unprecedented opportunities to integrate detailed GIS data into the heart of their business processes. Exposing services has dramatically expanded ESRI's customer base by providing a vehicle to put GIS information to work in virtually any context that has a need. In other words, putting tools in the hands of innovators has fueled business growth.

Organizations managing fleets of vehicles—such as trucking firms, emergency services, or police and security forces—are now able to integrate ESRI's real-time mapping data with GPS coordinates to track their members across the landscape. For the first time, they're able to simultaneously layer traffic flow, traffic accidents, and weather conditions onto the same maps—they're even able to simulate the impact of an earthquake.

The company's latest pilot project, for a pair of undisclosed cities, will marry GIS data about stoplight locations, and similar types of roadway infrastructure, with maintenance histories and supplier data, allowing the municipal governments of each city to detect patterns of wear-and-tear and change suppliers if one is proven to be especially ineffective. Melding those disparate sources of data would be impossible were it not for services.

Chapter *3*

Company and Customers

Upon deciding to rewrite Hugo Wunderkind's homegrown application and its clones around a suite of services (and tossing out their original, rickety code), it doesn't take long for Josh Lovecraft to set this plan in motion.

Within a few weeks, Wunderkind's original tool has been moved off his personal blog and onto Vorpal's web site, where it's been rebuilt by Lovecraft's developers and officially dubbed "PopMe!" The NC State chapter of Delta Rho Upsilon promptly rewrote their own application in just three days, once Vorpal made the same services available for outside use and once Delta Rho Upsilon's CompSci majors rose to the challenge. Their version ("PopX!") quickly propagated to Delta Rho Upsilon chapters across the country, and within a week, more than 40 fraternities were running the new, more stable application—all under a terms and conditions agreement created by Vorpal that indemnified the company against abuse.

With the pilot application up and running, and a steady stream of PopMe!-Matic orders pouring in, Vorpal is preparing similar applications for its other market verticals. But before Lovecraft and his team can do that, the company and its executives must first answer a larger question: how to structure the customer relationship within the context of these applications? How will the company address all of the opportunities unearthed by "PopMe!'s" success with a strategy that brings together technology, marketing, pricing, security practices, and more?

That's exactly what today's meeting with Jane Moneymaker, Josh Lovecraft, and David Wannamaker, Vorpal's VP of marketing, is set to address.

Forget the Web

"...We already have our own portal, and our content management systems are capable of handling it," Wannamaker says, leaning back in his chair at Moneymaker's conference table. "They were designed to produce our product catalogs, so it would be easy to generate a unique ID for every customized product they create. We'll use that to create separate HTML pages on Vorpal's site for every PopMe! spin-off, and we've just started talks with Yahoo! about offering our customizers as part of the Geocities standard kits. The Geocities folks are psyched—this is really cutting edge stuff for them—and their bosses further up the chain at Yahoo! are excited about the advertising prospects for the whole thing..."

"David, that's great," Moneymaker interrupts, "but it sounds all too familiar, this is right out of our old online playbook. I think what Hugo has done, and what the college students have done, is something quite different, isn't it?"

"What do you mean?" asks Wannamaker, confused.

"The application as it exists now is just one environment designed to customize Pop-Matics and order them through our web services APIs, but now you're saying we should sort of break it up a little bit and turn it into a web site?" Moneymaker asks.

"Well... yeah, I am," Wannamaker says. "We've invested a lot of money in the portal and content tools, and this is what we do. And while it's great that a lot of fraternities have already embraced the Pop-Matic Customizer, once we reach a deal with Yahoo!, we're pretty much set for distribution..."

"But when we do that—*if* we do that—won't Yahoo! cover those sites in ads?"

"Yeah, that's how it works," Wannamaker replies, a little incredulously. "They're ad supported sites. That's how they generate revenue, and we're negotiating for our own cut..."

"David, can you bring up Yahoo! quickly on your laptop," Moneymaker interrupts again. "I want to show you something." Wannamaker, now more confused than ever, and looking a little angry, dutifully opens his laptop and types the URL. "Search for 'popcorn makers'," she commands. Wannamaker does just that, and when he hits return, an ad appears for Vorpal's top competitor.

"What's the ad for?" Moneymaker asks.

"Well, it's for a competing product," Wannamaker says.

"Exactly. I want to build solutions that retain our customers—not send them into the arms of our competitors. Don't you think they're purchasing the ad words for 'popcorn', or banners, or whatever, and running ads to people searching for Vorpal? How much of the work we spend on building this relationship with our customers will be hijacked by the competition because we don't control the environment? What's our web retention rate now? Five percent? One percent?"

"Well, it happens to everybody," Wannamaker counters.

"Yes it does, but this time, it's happening to us," Moneymaker says evenly, looking him dead in the eye, "and I would rather that didn't happen. We're the ones who are going to lose the attention of our customers if we do this. So why do we have to? Why not do what the fraternities have done and create another immersive environment for our customers? Doesn't our retention rate get better when we're the preferred, or even the only option around?"

"Jane, I totally see where you're coming from in theory," Wannamaker offers, "but in practice, I'm working with the web tools I've been given, that we spent millions on and that I spent five years learning to optimize."

"Well, maybe we should stop spending those millions and not just do what we've always done with the Web and start making money," she responds. "Maybe we should take more of a leap, as Hugo and all of these outsiders have done." She turns her attention to Lovecraft, who has sat silently, thinking, during her exchange with Wannamaker. "Why don't we create an environment that we control, that reduces our ever growing Web management costs and allows us to avoid interference from our competitors and keeps the signal-to-noise ratio down?"

"When I first saw Hugo's application, I thought it was a broken toy," Lovecraft says. "But after a few months of research, I'm pretty sold on the potential of tools like the PopMe! engine. The Web is changing. It isn't about browsers any more. Through these mashups and the services that make them possible, the Web is becoming a platform for transacting business. Our APIs enable anyone to 'mashup' with our systems, whether they're web-based or not. And they're not toys. They're real applications—a special case of a larger concept called composite applications. There's no real reason we can't create our own tools, with our own interfaces, for customizing our own products—or to give our more expert customers the power to do the same thing from the business systems or sites. Either way, we're engaged in transacting business, not re-finding customers we've already found."

"Wait a second," Wannamaker says, trying desperately to get a handle on all of this. "What's the HTML for then? Do you really want to bypass the portal tool altogether?"

"Not at all," Moneymaker says. "The web site is an on-ramp, perhaps the easiest route to get customers downloading our applications, using our APIs, or extending our business reach by mashing up our applications with theirs. And once our customers implement them, we've got them. And once we've got them, they're going to discover a user experience and business environment that's a hell of a lot better than what's out there on the Web right now."

Moneymaker picks up her phone and points the receiver at Wannamaker and Lovecraft. "I'm going to get Hugo on the phone and see what he thinks of this, and whether he has any ideas concerning composite applications or mashups to our APIs."

A few rings later and Hugo Wunderkind is on speaker in her office. "Hugo, this is what we're thinking," Moneymaker says. "We're thinking we should take the focus off Vorpal's own web site and seed versions of PopMe! across the Web. Josh calls them 'mashups'."

"Wow! That's great," Hugo says, his excitement piercing the static. "This is totally synchronicity. We've been hatching a bunch of prototype mashups down here for the last three weeks."

"Really?" Lovecraft says.

"Sure," Hugo says. "We've been working on all sorts of stuff along those lines, and most of it has nothing to do with printing labels on individual products. We've come up with a mashup application for interior designers to help them visualize what Vorpal products would look like in the context of their projects; we made another for architects so they can account for the kitchen space needed while they're still drawing up blueprints. And the one we're working on right now draws upon the catalog—start with a generic kitchen and then customize it with Vorpal products drawn straight from the current version. Once they've finished designing the room, they can check out with one click, or create an online gift registry with everything in it—all kinds of stuff!"

"You're not doing all of this on your own, are you?" Lovecraft asks with a shocked look on his face. "Where are you getting the expertise to do this? And the resources? Why wasn't I told about this?"

"They're way too complicated for us to build on our own down here in marketing, Josh," Hugo says, sounding chastened, "but we're scoping them out right now and we were going to give you a call in a week or so about helping us out."

"Let's meet later today in my office to discuss this," Lovecraft suggests, feeling as if he's starting to get a handle on the situation.

"Well, this all feels right to me," Moneymaker says. "Let's keep pursuing this mashup strategy and see where it takes us. But let's not lose sight of the need to prove the PopMe! pilot project, get it into production, and start making money."

"It doesn't feel right to me," Wannamaker grumbles. "We've just gotten proficient with our current tools, so of course it's time to ditch everything again..."

▉ Rules

The rules below stem from breaking what was once an untouchable rule: that the eBusiness web site was the best way to broadly engage in business with customers on the Internet. That has led to an extremely competitive and costly web experience offering customers the freedom of self-service web forms and information queries. It also brings the unfortunate baggage of your competitors constantly trying to piggyback upon and hijack your customer relationships. It's time to rethink the rules governing your web strategy in the context of SOA.

Rule:
Browsers Browse, Services Transact

Services represent the raw materials to execute business transactions. Despite all of HTML's great virtues associated with providing a ubiquitous user interface (we wouldn't have the Web without it), building transactional capabilities inside web sites is costly and doesn't scale efficiently.

In other words, SOA APIs separate the business transaction from the user interface, thus enabling services to transact business with any number of applications, other services or composite user interfaces without needing any modification. By contrast, HTML-based web applications act as a gateway to transaction systems and must be centrally adapted and supported to bring aboard each new customer, environment, product, etc. These hidden costs and the labor associated with constantly maintaining and changing web sites to accommodate the changing business environment can be substantially reduced via services. Because they are not designed in the context of their user interface, creative companies can streamline the cost of engaging customers, which amounts to using web sites and HTML to inform and expose the services handling the actual transactions.

Solutions targeting browsers also suffer from the flaws of passivity and interruptability, which is to say that it's difficult to control the experience. What if the user doesn't return or is being bombarded with banner ads, popups, etc.? In practice, this means that competitors frequently interrupt your web conversations with customers via their own ads.

Switching to a service-oriented interface in a composite application enables you to keep control of the conversation. Transactional interfaces help solidify customer loyalty by establishing direct and ongoing business links. Think of it as the difference between searching for a supplier while being interrupted by advertising (30-second television ads, or popups) and utilizing a preferred supplier paid through a corporate account. Instead of wooing your customers continually in a bid just to keep their attention, have them transact directly with your services or a trusted partner's instead. Woo them once and lock them in.

Rule:
Automate the Unnecessary

Humans are the weakest point in the system; look to use services to support and enable them. We know that we are a persistent source of unreliability. In the same vein as the previous rule, this one is meant as a reminder that, too often, online forms ask people to fill in (and re-fill) information or to make associations that make sense to a machine but not to them. With services, we must do better.

Services can establish links to additional services offering related information. For instance, an application linked to your customer database might automatically fill-in every field with minimal effort from the user—or eliminate certain forms altogether—thus reducing errors, labor time and cost, or perhaps that last, crucial iota of resistance to a purchase. Using services, you have the power to make the underlying technology support the desired richness of your customer's experience. Ever more information is becoming available electronically from RFID tags, sensor networks, computing devices (such as GPS location) or other services, making the creative reduction of unnecessary and error-prone human data entry possible and desirable.

Rule:
Services Retain Customers

Beyond the cost savings and automation benefits of the previous pair of rules, there is also the notion that SOA can be a powerful tool for retaining and rewarding customers. Composite applications make direct, personalized customer engagements both compelling and desirable. Repeat business becomes seamless with previously defined processes and business agreements enforced through services. Forget remembering user-IDs, passwords, or customer and loyalty numbers. Once a customer has linked their business or personal services with yours, they'll prefer the more secure and private benefits of composite solutions versus entering their favorite URL or performing a web search to return to your site. Privacy, security, efficiency and service quality become new value propositions for the customer. Not only will they look more favorably upon their interactions with your brands, but also your competitors are no longer lurking within the same browser window.

■ Putting the Rules to Work

To put composite applications to work effectively it is important to have a complete understanding and prepare at both the architectural and legal levels.

Mashups and Composite Applications

A "mashup" is the trendy name for simple web applications created from combining two or more services. The name comes from pop music, where professional DJs and talented amateurs alike have made a hobby out of mashing up multiple, disparate songs to create new sounds.

Mashups are the most popular and easily understood examples of composite applications, which draw upon web services and other sources of functionality to create entirely new features. (See the Appendix for a ground up explanation of SOA and the crucial role that composite applications play.) Mashups are also the simplest and most accessible form of composites, as they tend to be created using data and features from publicly available sources like Google, Amazon.com, eBay, Windows Live and Yahoo! They often require only a passing familiarity with the underlying code, and thus mashups are often created by unlikely innovators who create value by combining and recombining existing services and data in unprecedented ways.

Google is widely given credit for kick starting the mashup phenomenon for creating the Google Maps API, a service which lets anyone utilize the company's software and database for rendering customized maps of their own. Using the Google Maps API is as simple as creating what's called an "API Key" which binds the service to your own web site and data set, then creating a map interface using simple JavaScript. The end results look like the Chicago Crime map, in which instances of violent crimes are mapped to the city's street grid. Other instances include numerous maps charting real estate data, while more frivolous uses include mapping the birthplaces of Oscar winners and even American Idol contestants.

Mashups are important in the context of SOA because they've already shown the value of what services can provide. They're the public face of the larger composite application structures made possible by an SOA.

Mashups and larger composites alike are what are called "**service consumers**," applications, which draw upon services for their functionality. The underlying applications powering those services are known as "**service providers**." The creation of services, the birth of composites, and the recasting of enterprise software as service providers, were all made possible by the transformation of the traditional application stack to an SOA version, which is also explained in the Appendix. The special advantages of services (including mashups) over traditional enterprise applications is shown in Figure 3-1:

Traditional Enterprise Software

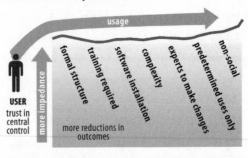

Enterprise Web 2.0 Software

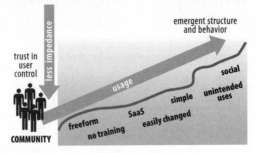

Figure 3.1: Advantages of Services over Traditional Applications[1]

But focusing too much on the novelty and power of emerging Web 2.0 solutions is making a big mistake. To gain the maximum business advantage from SOA, it is important to keep in mind that services transform the Web from a centralized HTML-based

---

[1] This graphic was adapted from Dion Hinchcliffe's blog (http://blogs.zdnet.com/Hinchcliffe/?p=57) which was inspired by Andrew McAfee's article: "Enterprise 2.0: The Dawn of Emergent Collaboration," *MIT Sloan Management Review* Spring 2006.

platform into a service-based platform that opens up the means of executing transactions to a whole new audience. Web 2.0 solutions, including mashups, may be one of the first ways that this value is being delivered, but they won't be the end of the story.

A Legal and Engineering Framework for SOA

As your SOA efforts begin to mature, drawing more and more third parties into your service-enabled ecosystem, it will gradually become necessary to replace ad hoc, case-by-case rules and service user support with a more consistent, structured framework. A few steps in the evolution of that framework may include:

1. **A standard legal agreement outlining the terms of services and rules of use for the services you provide.** Software makers are no strangers to issuing terms of service for every piece of code they offer to the world, but all other companies will want to explore the legal issues involved in providing services and draft a comprehensive, legally binding agreement for anyone seeking to participate.

2. **Documentation for the semantics of the services being offered.** It's one thing to offer services as bare-boned pieces of functionality, but it's difficult to expect anyone to produce dazzling results if they lack the understanding of how these services fit into your larger business, and what data they're drawing upon. Some documentation explaining what these services do in the greater scheme of things is absolutely

necessary, although offering just enough detail to entice developers while shielding your secrets from the world is an art unto itself. Providing examples of how to use services is crucial.

3. **A developer community site or other structure to assist third parties in communicating with you and with each other.** Again, software companies are no strangers to development forums and supporting rich online communities, but everyone else will eventually need to create a communal destination for sharing advice, results, news, and information about the services being offered and the individuals working with them. It doesn't make much sense to attempt to grow a community of developers around your services if you won't provide the support infrastructure for them.

4. **Technical support and additional help for developers.** Your outside innovators won't always be able to put their heads together to solve their problems. Increased service usage will demand some kind of technical support operation that can rapidly respond to developers enquiries and calls for help.

■ Examples

Each of these examples demonstrates how composite applications create value through new transactional environments built from services provided by others. Notice how general-purpose services are adapted to meet the needs of specific contexts.

Elephant Drive

Elephant Drive is an example of an enterprise mashup focused on a back-office operational problem. The company offers a network-based and mobility-friendly backup service that incorporate Amazon's Simple Storage Service (S3) and Intel's Mobility Software Development Kit (SDK). The idea for the company sprang from a conversation between the two founders, Michael Fisher and Ben Widhelm, who realized that all of the photographs of the first year of Ben's son's life lay vulnerable on the hard drive of his wife's laptop. If that drive failed or if the laptop were lost or stolen...poof, no pictures. Michael and Ben imagined that a huge market existed for a backup service that was simple, easy-to-use, and affordable.

After researching the available consumer-focused alternatives and finding them either annoyingly complex or "technically bankrupt", Michael and Ben realized that there was ample room for a new solution that could automate the unnecessary, provide an engaging user experience through services and gain an edge by supporting mobility. Both men had been through start-ups before—they knew it would be critical to maximize their resources so they could keep as much of the company in their hands as possible. One surefire way to do that was to avoid large expenses as long as possible until revenue was coming in.

As they started creating the software in early 2005, they observed that cheap storage over the network was an inevitability.

Some company that had built a huge complex of data centers—Google, Yahoo!, Microsoft, IBM—would eventually seek revenue by selling network-accessible storage at wholesale rates. The key would be to create a simple application that could capitalize on that storage service. Virtually as soon as Michael and Ben started development, they were pleasantly surprised to find that Amazon was the first large-scale storage service provider. Its S3 service offered storage for 15 cents per gigabyte per month, with a 20 cent per gigabyte fee per incoming and outgoing transfer.

Once they set to creating the client-side application that would allow data to be transferred from a desktop or laptop it became clear that support for mobile users was a must. The normal person may be disconnected from a high speed Internet connection for days at a time, or on the move and away from power supplies. Using the Intel Mobility SDK, Michael and Ben made the Elephant Drive software sensitive to the mobility context of the laptop. The software avoids performing backups when the battery is low or the network connection is slow. The thresholds and events that affect the software can be tuned by the user.

Elephant Drive has been live for 7 months as of August, 2006, and has more than 10,000 users. The company is still in its public beta phase and has done virtually no marketing. In the fourth quarter of 2006, Michael and Ben will solicit for many more users and will eventually offer a fee-based service, selling 10 gigabytes of backup for about $9.95 a month and 50 gigabytes for $20 per month. They plan on offering accounts of 1 gigabyte or less for free.

Ben and Michael both agree that services have profoundly changed the landscape for entrepreneurs and businesses in a way that will lead to a parade of new products. Amazon's S3 and the Intel Mobility SDK are both highly valuable, general-purpose offerings that were just waiting to be put to use in the right context. Ben and Michael understood a context for a product that could create value, and they leveraged the services to rapidly create a new offering at a fraction of what it would have cost just five years ago. Ben and Michael have realized that they can benefit from offering services as well as consuming them. They plan on opening up their API as services so that other developers can create products they are not focused on or help to extend the reach of their offerings, such as backup clients for Linux, the Mac, and even handheld devices.

SmugMug/S3

SmugMug is an online photo-sharing service with 15 employees, 150,000 customers, and 72 million photos in its effectively limitless database. It's one of a rapidly growing number of companies leveraging Amazon.com's Simple Storage Service (S3) as the foundation for its own offerings.

S3 is essentially a web service-enabled extension of the company's massively scalable data storage infrastructure, which Amazon has chosen to commoditize at wholesale rates. The service uses REST-based and SOAP-based interfaces designed to work with any basic internet development toolkit, and currently offers HTTP and BitTorrent as its download protocols. It's designed to be simple, cheap, and infinitely scalable, and a raft of startups—including ElephantDrive, Altexa, Jungle Disk, MediaSilo, Ookles, Plum, and SmugMug—have already signed up.

The advantages of enterprise-class storage-as-a-service are obvious to heavy users. SmugMug saved $500,000 over just three months by using S3 instead of adding new servers. Currently growing at a rate of 10 terabytes worth of photos each month, that's an extra cost of just $1,500 using S3. By comparison, a 7-terabyte RAID server costs about $13,000.

The result is a win-win relationship for both SmugMug and Amazon. The former has access to an immense storage platform it neither had to pay to build nor amortize, while Amazon has been able to turn one of its biggest IT costs into a revenue generator.

Associate-O-Matic

Another web service-enabled application that enables new forms of selling of the sort Vorpal is pursuing is "Associate-O-Matic," a menu-based toolkit for rapidly assembling Amazon Associate storefronts. Amazon Associates are independent web site operators such as GadgetMadness.com or DVDPulse.com, which have created customized interfaces for selling Amazon's products. Rather than build their own e-commerce infrastructures, they outsource the entire process, receiving only a commission from each sale in exchange for essentially driving customers to Amazon.

In 2003, a developer and entrepreneur named Justin Mecham used Amazon-offered services to create a pair of online stores,

TVmojo.com and WirelessMojo.com. The code he wrote for developing these sites became the foundation of the Associate-O-Matic, which automates the creation of these storefronts using bundled services. The full-featured version, which costs $99 per license, comes complete with Amazon's shopping cart, search functionality, currency conversion, and total integration with the etailer's American, U.K., and Canadian stores. Users are guided through simple web page creation routines that describe how items for sale will appear on the screen, and 150 additional settings are all controlled via a browser-based control panel. No programming and no databases are required.

More than 6,000 copies of the Associate-O-Matic have been downloaded to date, each one representing a new stream of revenue for a fledgling retailer and a new sales channel for Amazon.

US Department of Health and Human Services/Grants.gov

Grants.gov is a U.S. Federal "e-Government" initiative designed to simplify and integrate what were fragmented, time-consuming, inconsistent, and paper-intensive processes. The result is a one-stop portal where individuals and organizations can apply electronically for grants from any of the federal government's 26 grant-making agencies, which dole out a combined $400 billion annually.

As one of the largest grant dispensers, the Department of Health and Human Services (HHS) was asked to spearhead the project. Seeking to balance the needs of varied and competing agencies, HHS faced an architectural decision immediately: whether to deploy downloadable, online/offline XML forms that users complete on their own, or provide an HTML interface that keeps users tied to the site while completing the applications. HHS chose the former.

To use the forms, users download them from the site, and then fill them out through a downloadable PC-based intelligent document reader. When completed, the forms are submitted to an SOA-based API. By using online/offline XML forms HHS is able to avoid standardizing around a single form (which would have brought it into conflict with other agencies) and lower costs by decreasing the load and maintenance that a real-time HTML-based interface would have required. Using XML allows every agency to use unique forms, while automating the collection, sharing, and analysis of the information from completed forms. And with the advancements in intelligent document technology, logic being embedded into the grant forms can make filling out the form offline as interactive as would be expected of online systems.

And now grant-seeking organizations are able to connect their own grants management systems with the Grants.gov agency systems using XML-based services making the solution "multi-lingual". This feature increases accuracy and saves the time otherwise spent manually re-entering data into forms. Allowing applicants to store incomplete forms (which may run into the hundreds of pages) on their own servers also decreases Grants.gov's costs and lessens worries about protecting data.

The services used in the Grants.gov architecture reduces costs by promoting reuse. In the traditional web HTML model, each new grant would require a team of developers to build the pages and integrate them with the appropriate database, etc. With the SOA workflow in place however, development costs are limited to creating only what is needed to support the new aspects of a form. In essence a one-time cost to develop the service oriented system replaces the recurring labor and support costs of building online interactive solution through traditional methods.

Chapter 4

Suppliers and IT

Six weeks after CEO Jane Moneymaker's decision to gear up a makeshift PopMe!-Matic assembly line and seek customers, the orders that have poured in since have resoundingly confirmed her suspicions that there is a real market here after all. But the initial success of the customized poppers has created its own problems.

Because of Moneymaker's decision to fulfill orders during this pilot using a process that could charitably be described as "ad hoc," the quick ramp-up in order volume has begun to wreak havoc on Vorpal's Pop-Matic supply chain. Scaling production of the mass of customized poppers seems impossible, because each order demands that a unique decal be printed and applied by hand to each appliance. The mounting frustration caused by this interruption on the assembly line has made Moneymaker and her team truly appreciate the typically invisible efficiency of the company's suppliers.

Today, three of Moneymaker's lieutenants—CIO Josh Lovecraft, VP of Marketing David Wannamaker, and Vorpal's VP of Operations, Wendy Chiselpenny—are having a meeting with David Quartermaster, the EVP of sales for Emblazon, the decal/transfer supplier that Vorpal turned to in the wake of its private label deal with Target. While Vorpal's side of the table has a distinct aura of urgency bordering on desperation, Quartermaster resembles the proverbial cat that ate the canary.

"...I know how to buy 100,000 units of something, and I know how to buy 1 million units of something," Chiselpenny is saying, "and I can squeeze the best price out of the guy across the table every time—present company excluded of course," she says, nodding to Quartermaster. "But now I'm being asked to buy something one at a time, and this is a whole new ball game for us to work through together. I'm hoping you can tell me how to make that happen."

"Oh, we understand your problem, all right," Quartermaster says. "We've been selling customized decals[1] for our other customers for a while now, and we had terrible problems at first trying to build something resembling an efficient process. It took us a

---

[1] The word "decals" is used in the United States for what are known as "transfers" in other parts of the world. See the sidebar in Chapter 1 for a brief note on the two terms.

good six months of fumbling around before we hit upon the idea of adapting our services to allow each customer to include their customer decal definitions as part of their order. Essentially, they directly route orders from their systems to our printing facilities. Now we basically appear to their systems as an enormous, virtual, laser printer—the industrial equivalent of having a printer icon on your desktop. You send us a stream of images for custom decals and you get back a roll of decals that can be automatically affixed in your plant. Each roll has a unique ID, which is used in a service call that tells which order is in which position on the roll. The tools we're supplying smaller customers—such as configuration applications similar to the one you cooked up—and Intelligent Documents that we send out to customers as customized order forms are all done through the same services.

"Adhering to an SOA has pretty much ended the hassle, because our customers have their choice of how to interface through our services to help us print whatever they need with minimal assistance from us—and that has driven down both of our costs."

"That sounds quite do-able," Josh Lovecraft says. "We should be able to begin routing XML-wrapped requests with our orders almost immediately. We'll need to extend our manufacturing process to include a few new services first, but that shouldn't be difficult. How quickly can you get the XML and WSDL formats, posting options, etc. to our people? "

"That's great, but it's not enough," Quartermaster interrupts. "The web services information and definitions are on our corporate site, but that won't solve the problem on its own."

"What do you mean?" Lovecraft asks.

"I think you understand how important it is to follow our guidelines on how to design your order mechanisms efficiently so you're passing us all the data we need in the format we need. We've taken a look at your PopMe! applications, and think we can improve certain aspects of it to make it mesh a little better with our production systems. There're two more things.

"One, our main facility is in Memphis, and I know you make the majority of your Pop-Matics in Malaysia. Considering that we're both near FedEx hubs, processing your last orders of the day and syncing them with our system immediately, our late shift could be processing those orders and have them back on the truck to the airport the same night, instead of having our day shift discover those orders the next day. Do you see what I mean?

"The second thing is a little similar. We need you to communicate with us, and not just send us orders. If you can tell us about the intricacies of your production process—which plants are the ones where the PopMe!-Matics are being produced, and how time elapses between your decal order and when it needs to be applied, etc.—we can sync up the printing and delivery of our products to match yours. That means less inventory for both sides, lower costs... you see where I'm going with this, right?"

"Absolutely," replies Chiselpenny. "And the last thing we need are warehouses filled with one-off decals meant for one customer and one customer alone."

"Exactly," Quartermaster says, nodding sagely. "So we have some services we'd like you to use—services that will do a decent job integrating your production systems with our own. If you're uncomfortable downloading the information from our site, or want to establish a dedicated or more secure link, I'll have our IT guys prepare some documentation for Vorpal—we're increasingly doing this with all our customers, so we have templates already prepared.

"Oh, and there's one other thing," Quartermaster says, dropping his voice to a low, conspiratorial tone. "We already print a lot of custom decals for markets you've never thought about, and we have relationships in these markets that go back for years."

"Like who?" Wannamaker says, practically jumping out of his chair.

"We've made inroads into the surfing and skateboard subcultures—there's a huge aftermarket in both when it comes to personalization. I bet both of those—and that's just two out of a few dozen market niches we serve—could be prime targets for your popcorn poppers and just about everything else you sell."

"The 'Tony Hawk Pop-Matic'," Wannamaker says dreamily to no one in particular. "I can already see it now... But who are you selling to in that market? Could you introduce us to someone like

Burton or Quiksilver so we could sell our products on their sites? If we could tap into the channels you already have in place, we could both boost our sales considerably…" he muses.

The meeting quickly wraps up with a promise to exchange services and data, and to connect Emblazon and Vorpal's production systems more effectively than any supplier that had come before.

"…Usually my job is to leave my suppliers a smoking ruin and walk away with the best possible deal in hand," Wendy Chiselpenny half-jokingly tells Quartermaster on his way out, "but this meeting didn't follow that script at all."

With a Cheshire cat grin on his face, Quartermaster nods again. "Yes, we've noticed that as soon as we created our new services and started doing mass customization for our customers, the relationship changed pretty quickly from a Darwinian struggle to a win-win situation—from conflict to collaboration, if you will—because we're both going to make a lot more money that way. I like to think of it as negotiation jujitsu—it's now my job to use your strength to create new business for us instead of just holding the line on price while you pummel me."

■ Rules

From an SOA perspective, empowering your suppliers isn't that much different from empowering your customers and outside innovators, and the rewards can be just as great. The rules below are guidelines for establishing a new relationship between your company and its suppliers that stresses collaboration and mutual success rather than simply walking away with the best price possible.

Rule:
Suppliers are Services

Redefine the advantages that suppliers can deliver through your business. Just as services enable innovators on the far side of the firewall to experiment and add value to your efforts to reach customers, SOA also has the capability to transform your relationships with suppliers. By defining these relationships as a set of reusable services, it becomes much easier to add new suppliers and switch between them more easily, adding a new degree of flexibility that has been missing in rigid, cost-defined relationships. While many suppliers are not yet service-enabled, establishing the SOA APIs you expect to use now will accelerate their adoption and create stronger business ties.

By the same token, solicit your suppliers for their best ideas and best efforts in much the same way you would turn to outside innovators. Invite them to improve your mutual processes, knowing that successfully doing so will be a win for both sides.

Rule:
Relationships are a Two-Way Street

Work with suppliers to directly add operational advantages through win-win processes. Related to the rule above, don't just define your suppliers as services—define your own operations as services to them. Reject the Darwinian model that currently exists—where only one supplier can win out over the others, and its "reward" is to have its margins squeezed mercilessly by customers—and replace it with a collaborative model built on services. Information shared in this way then becomes the foundation for continual process improvement, as static forecasting and manufacturing processes slowly give way to newly discovered market opportunities and new response mechanisms—just like Hugo Wunderkind's discovery and invention of the PopMe!-Matic.

Rule:
Everyone can be a Channel

See your suppliers as channels to new markets via their own eco-systems. Your suppliers have more customers than you know, who might, in theory, become your customers as well. Not that your suppliers have been inclined to share them when your relationship amounted to placing said suppliers in a vise. But as part of the transition from a winner-takes-all to a win-win relationship, your suppliers will become a new sales channel in the form of their customers and their customers' customers. Elaborating on the rule: combining your and your supplier's services cooperatively can establish much stronger win-win value propositions that make compelling business sense to the ultimate paying customers.

Rule:
Services are Multi-lingual

Don't insist on only using your internal 'standards'; recognize the benefit of increased external flexibility. As noted above in the first rule, using services to connect and define partner relationships enables your company to add new suppliers more smoothly and at only a fraction of current costs. Use this capability to support many different methods of transacting, rather than just one—offering the benefits of choice can lead to creative customer solutions, cost savings, and extending the reach of your services. Emblazon created one set of services, but allowed the customer to develop their own "languages" for interfacing with them. Larger companies may have CRM or ERP systems they may choose to integrate as well.

Even simpler solutions are quickly emerging. Small businesses or even individuals might use intelligent documents embedded with XML information. Adobe Interactive Forms and others now process and submit information from their documents as web service calls. This makes it very easy for the novice user who only needs to provide customers with documents to submit, which the application does by essentially "phoning home" upon submission. And then there are Flash and other composite application environments, which generate rich user interfaces that can be linked back into the same services. Vorpal's SOA affords a rich set of services to support many different types of usage as shown in Figure 4-1:

Traditional Web Model

SOA Services Are Multi-Lingual**

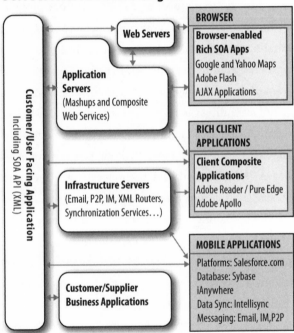

** Other brands and names are the property of their respective owners.

Figure 4-1: Vorpal's SOA options vs. Traditional HTML Solution

Rule:
Empower Your Ecosystem

All of the above rules lead to this one: think of your partners and suppliers as members of a dynamic ecosystem: yours.

Harvard Business School professor Marco Iansiti has coined the term "the Keystone Advantage" to describe how companies can leverage the network of companies (an ecosystem) surrounding them. Iansiti (who has since co-written a book on the subject) drew his insights from biology, in which "keystone species" proactively maintain the health of their entire ecosystem for the ultimately self-serving reason that their own survival depends on it.

But survival is a two-way-street—those supporting species depend upon the keystone to flourish in much the same way that an actual arch cannot stand if the keystone is removed.

In a business setting, your company is probably one among many that functions as a keystone for your suppliers. Your goal should be to create and enlarge your company's own ecosystem, taking care to reward members and actively encourage others to join. Not only will your company gain competitive leverage from having the largest, most flourishing ecosystem on the block, but over time the ecosystem itself might become a business opportunity, as other companies might turn to you to outsource functions your ecosystem is better equipped to handle.

■ Putting the Rules to Work

Applying these rules means creating a new world for you and your suppliers, one in which your communication is intermediated by services. This requires new levels of standardization and changes relationships quite profoundly.

The Vision of "The Real-Time Enterprise"

Our collective efforts to squeeze waste, eliminate inefficiency, accelerate the flow of information and the speed of decision-making, and integrate business processes into a single, seamless chain, all point toward an ideal state that's commonly called the "real-time enterprise."

In the vision of the real-time enterprise, process automation and fully integrated applications combine to offer a continuous, 360-degree view of the enterprise, its operations, and even its partners' and suppliers' operations. Individual corporations knit themselves together into partner ecosystems in which data freely passes across corporate boundaries. The goals of these ecosystems is the same of any business—discover new opportunities, cut costs, and please customers using new, better, fresher data originating everywhere and automatically sorted to the right people at the right time. From a competitive perspective, companies that move quickly and forcefully enough to create these ecosystems will have powerful leverage over those who don't. (Witness Wal-Mart and its relentless demands of its partners for ever-greater supply-chain integration.)

In this context, service-oriented architectures are seen as the next evolutionary step toward an IT architecture capable of supporting the vision. The flexible natures of services and composite applications lend themselves well to the idea of creating and reformulating business processes as needed to create these integrations. But what does this mean in practice? And what are the actual business benefits of doing so?

To answer that question, consider the meat and poultry industry. Seriously. The producers and "manufacturers" in those industries are formulating a set of XML standards for the storage and transfer of metadata concerning each and every one of their animals. The reason? In the age of "Mad Cow," hoof-and-mouth, and other diseases, the Japanese government, the European Union, and many other nations require that the origin and delivery of these animals to consumers be accounted for at every step in the process—from the supermarket or hypermarket back to the distribution center, to the meat packer, to the slaughterhouse, and so on, all the way back to the farm.

The intensity of this regulatory pressure has forced the producers in those industries to adopt a set of standards as a first step toward creating a universal set of services and business processes capable of tracking the status of a cow, a pig, or a chicken in real time through the production process in order to head off disease. This pressure isn't dissimilar to the pressure felt by any company in any industry to provide fresher and more detailed information about its products, whether the entity requesting that information is a government agency, the dominant partner in an ecosystem, or the end consumer herself.

A second source of pressure, in this case on IT, is the tremendous quantities of data produced in a system such as this. Attempting to keep track of every single animal at every single point in the global meatpacking production process is an incredible undertaking. So is tracking 46,000 trucks on the world's highways and byways, which is exactly what Wal-Mart intends to do using General Electric's VeriWise™ satellite telematics system.

Data volume at those kinds of scale will quickly overwhelm the classical enterprise application model of writing to traditional databases, recovering data, and taking it out again. The strain is already apparent in supply chain management systems, where developments like vendor-managed inventory (VMI) already put pressure on companies to respond in near real-time to inventory data.

Clearly, new data structures will be built on the edges for the rapid gathering, filtering, and discarding of this data without having to continually write and rewrite to hub systems. One such solution is known as "event-driven architecture," in which elaborate rules and key performance indicators automate and regulate the flow and sorting of data, requiring human attention only when an exceptional result (either exceptionally good or exceptionally bad) requires immediate intervention. And the best mechanisms available for creating such structures are services and composite applications.

The Role of Standards in an SOA

Standardization is a hot button topic in any industry, but this book takes the position that there are only two types of standards, essentially: any standard that is relevant to the success of group or industry in question is good, and any standard that isn't relevant to success is bad. With that in mind, the question companies should be asking each other is not "what standards do we have?" but rather, "do we want to do business together, and, if we do, then what standards do we adopt?"

Adoption is ultimately the issue, not standards acceptance or ratification. The software industry in particular is littered with standards that won official certification from the ISO and other industry bodies, only to be abandoned in the face of more widely adopted unofficial standards.

With that in mind, don't hesitate to create your own standards or to eagerly participate in standard-setting for your respective ecosystem. As always, the fastest and most dominant companies and organizations will drive the adoption of standards and the pace of change.

Using Your Suppliers as a Channel

The traditional relationship between a company and its suppliers is a thoroughly antagonistic one, with the former eternally angling to cut its costs, outsource assembly steps, and pass risk along to the suppliers, which win the Pyrrhic victory of its business. After decades of this, many companies have whittled away their suppliers to single sources that actually perform much of the manufacturing work in question before handing the components over for final assembly.

This model, which has successfully wrung billions of dollars and euros out of the supply chains of many a company, is not without costs elsewhere. Critics of globalization point to the inherent flaw of relying on only a few suppliers—any disruption, no matter how small, at any point in the chain, can have drastic consequences for all involved, including consumers.

But considering the competitive pressure in today's global market, coupled with the cost and complexity to onboard niche suppliers, such consolidation was inevitable. But those costs begin to shrink in an SOA environment.

As the examples of Vorpal and Emblazon illustrate above, service-enabled automated systems are much easier to set up—because linking services is much easier than attempting to integrate enterprise applications—and administrate, thanks to the increased visibility into each other's operations. In SOA-powered supplier relationships, it's much easier to imagine customer-supplier collaboration on component designs—to reduce risk and achieve greater efficiency—and efforts on the supplier's part to expand the market for both, as both will benefit.

The relationship ultimately becomes much less about reducing costs—because the costs to add or subtract suppliers gradually becomes minimized—and much more about reducing the risk for both and increasing flexibility. The company-supplier equation changes shape: instead of defining, and battling over, how much to produce at what price, they collaborate on how best to deliver value to the end customer, which is the heart of their businesses.

■ Examples

These examples show how new attitudes toward supplier relationships and new services can be a powerful force in harnessing the energy of an ecosystem of companies.

SalesForce.com

Salesforce.com is one of the initial Software as a Service (SaaS) success stories. Along with building his online CRM business, Marc Benioff, CEO choose to extend his platform to a broader ecosystem by introducing the AppExchange platform. The ecosystem has responded aggressively and now over 250 unique SaaS solutions are available. Equally significant, more than 50,000 custom objects and applications have been created by salesforce.com customers.

With each new generation of their core platform however, salesforce.com and other vendors are building and rebuilding capabilities to enable mobile users to access the salesforce.com platform. That all changed in early 2006 when salesforce.com acquired Sendia and its platform for enabling mobile solutions. In acquiring Sendia, salesforce.com provided a means for all users of the AppExchange platform to mobilize their applications. The platform users did not need to build mobile technology on their own as mobile technology is now provided by the platform.

The approach taken by salesforce.com highlights how services can be compounded to the greater benefit of customers. Using the infrastructure developed by salesforce.com, Benioff has enabled a passionate ecosystem that is rapidly developing and offering new on-demand services. Then, realizing that educating every solution developer on the idiosyncrasies of mobility was a daunting task limiting his business to the realm of those that are connected to the Internet, he provided his ecosystem a platform that "Mobilizes" the solutions running in the salesforce.com environment. Now with only a small amount of validation an application is certified to function with the saleforce.com mobile platform, providing consistency of user experience as well as opening up his market to the ever-increasing number of mobile users.

Lastminute.com

Lastminute.com is an online travel merchant that specializes, as its name would imply, in the sale of highly perishable plane tickets, hotel rooms, vacation packages, and other travel- and tourism-related commodities poised to expire. The company's business model is based on an inversion of typical travel planning, in which the customer chooses dates and a destination, and then seeks the best combination of price and features that conform to their criteria.

In the case of Lastminute.com's offers, the timing is a hard parameter—availability is more or less immediate—and rather than wait for potential customers to seek destinations on its site, the company continually offers deals and packages via email to the nearly 10 million subscribers. Over the last eight years, Lastminute. com has aggregated approximately 13,600 suppliers—the aforementioned airlines, hotels, etc.—all of which pass information on expiring seats or rooms to Lastminute.com for packaging and selling.

The result is a neat arbitrage of the fixed-time weakness of the travel industry. All of these suppliers, faced with valuable inventory that perishes every night or even every hour, benefit by recruiting Lastminute.com's customers. In turn, Lastminute.com has built a business on simply leveraging its supplier and customer relationships into a near real-time conversation about heavily discounted travel products. And, assuming their game is to go just about anywhere at the proverbial last minute, its customers pay very little for a great getaway.

Dell Inc.

Dell is justly famous for its supply chain process innovation, which the company rode to a 32 percent market share in the PC business despite major mergers by its rivals and only minimal spending on R&D. The secret of Dell's success is its leverage and its insight into its suppliers, which must be able, on a moment's notice, to deliver a batch of components to Dell within 90 minutes. But rather than simply tell its suppliers what to make and when to make it, Dell is able to see what it has in its own plant inventories on any given day, and then ask its supplier network to offer what they can provide and at what price they can provide it within say, the next 24 hours. In this way, Dell is able to "demand shape" customer orders by offering discounts to its customers on the same components that Dell purchased from the lowest bidder.

Rather than simply wait for its customers to tell it what computers it should be building, Dell searches for opportunities within its own supply chain and then convinces its customers what they should buy. While Dell's products have their fair share of critics, its supply chain optimization techniques transformed its sector, and have yet to be replicated by any of its competitors.

Chapter 5

IT and The Company

With the holiday rush over, Jane Moneymaker's executive team decided it was time to address the seismic shift that's taken place in the company since Hugo Wunderkind's online experiment was discovered by the world a few months before. By seizing that and other opportunities uncovered by further pilots, Vorpal has been able to speed its path to revenue. But in order to scale at the pace expected by this new generation of service-oriented applications, a transformation of how the company is organized will need to take place.

With services now playing a key role in the relationships between innovators, customers, suppliers, and the company, Vorpal must now change its internal IT organization and mandates in order to support this new generation of relationships properly.

Realizing this change was upon them, Moneymaker and Lovecraft met during the last week of the year and crafted a new charter for IT. It included a set of policies that took into account the fact that IT was no longer concerned with only the core business functions, but was also critical for enabling the revenue generating efforts at the line of business edges. During the peak of the holiday rush, Lovecraft had observed how the IT employees were grappling with the busiest online ordering days of the year, and he was amazed at how much homegrown innovation was hiding in the shadows. This "Shadow IT," as they had taken to calling it, was something Moneymaker wanted to bring out into the light. For his part, Lovecraft was a little afraid of what they might find.

Bringing "Shadow IT" Into the Light

On the first business day of the new year, Vorpal employees arrived at work to find an email waiting for them from their CEO.

Date: January 2, 2007, 07:16:23

From: Jane Moneymaker (jmoneymaker@vorpalinc.com)

To: Vorpal All

Subject: Time to Innovate

Good morning everyone;

I hope and trust that everyone had a fabulous holiday season and that you've recovered from the rush. I trust your friends

and family who received a Vorpal product as a gift this year
are as pleased with it as my father is with his Boston Red Sox
PopMe!-Matic.

Thank you for making this holiday one of our busiest and most
profitable.

I'm sure everyone in the company has begun to sense how
we're transforming how we do business. How we utilize ICT
within Vorpal is changing how we respond to our customers,
how we innovate internally, and how we share those
innovations with our suppliers.

I'm observing how those of you comfortable working with
new technologies have begun to take it upon yourselves to
quietly innovate new capabilities that help us achieve our
company's goals. I'm also acutely aware of the importance of
these "Shadow IT" projects to our ongoing success. By now,
most of you know how one of these "Shadow IT" efforts led
to the creation of PopMe!-Matics and ultimately to closing
deals last month with the National Football League and the
English Premier League. We are releasing the first officially
licensed sports appliances in history and I believe its success
will lead to portable versions of many more of our appliances
for vendors, tailgating, parties, picnics, and other outdoor
events in the second quarter of this year. All this sprang from

one person's great idea. We want to encourage all of you to innovate around your ideas while continuing to get our daily work done and, most of all, to meet our budgets and forecasts.

More importantly I've discovered that how we think about IT's role depends a great deal upon when each of us began our relationship with technology. As such, we're reorganizing a bit in order to more effectively encourage and integrate new capabilities into our official IT portfolio. The policies detailed in this email's attachments explain how we intend to take Shadow IT out of the shadows. Taking a page from Google's playbook, we're going to establish a corporate attitude that a percentage of each employee's time can be dedicated and self-directed into innovative projects. Our intent is to include everyone at Vorpal in creating and using new tools and services that can help us all in significant ways.

We're doing it to help ourselves continue to innovate rapidly while protecting our corporate information assets. Beyond your personal involvement we need to organize our ad hoc efforts in the following ways: 1) Ensuring you have the right tools. 2) Training you how to use them. 3) Retooling the areas where our IT systems have become a hindrance. 4) Converting our core business capabilities into an SOA. 5) Exposing more services to customers. 6) Empowering mobile employees and

customers by mobilizing their user experiences. 7) Encouraging
self-organizing communities internally and with our customers
through wikis, blogs, RSS feeds, and other Web 2.0 features.
And, finally, 8) engrain in our core values innovative results
that include reliability, security, privacy, compliance, re-use,
and most of all—*safety* first.

If all of this sounds bewildering, it was to me at first too. Your
managers have been briefed and will begin working with you
to help you take advantage of these new policies. I've asked
Vorpal's Chief Information Officer, Josh Lovecraft, to chair a
steering committee tracking Vorpal's usage of services and
innovation practices. I expect him to ensure that you will
all receive the resources necessary to utilize new services,
become part of the innovate process, and facilitate best
practices around reliability, security, compliance, etc.

So far, we have a few services up and running, with more
under construction. I'm soliciting the entire company to be
part of what we do next. It's our great hope that more than
a few of the services some of you will create will end up
benefiting the entire company.

In the spirit of our new policies, the steering committee and I
will start blogging about our innovation practices to keep our

corporate community up to date. This message will be the first blog entry.

Happy New Year,

Jane Moneymaker
CEO
Vorpal Inc.

The Service-Enabled Staff

Moneymaker's email went over well at Vorpal, all things considered. Some employees were thrilled that tech support was now charged with supporting their pet projects; many others were nervous—did their careers now depend on dreaming up services? How were they supposed to tend to the day-to-day business when they were suddenly expected to become as proficient as hackers? There was some turmoil at first, but the message was sinking in and there was no going back.

A few weeks later, Moneymaker dropped in on a meeting of Josh Lovecraft's innovation steering committee to hear for herself what her employees had come up with so far.

"...Everywhere I go, I'm being buttonholed about ideas for services, and while I enjoy the attention, to be frank, it's making me a little nervous," Moneymaker tells the room. "While I want people to be thinking about these issues, what I don't need is a company full of miniature Hugo Wunderkinds chasing ideas that turn out to be terrible. I'm worried that we're sending the message that execution doesn't count as much as it used to, when in fact, the opposite is true."

Frank Cashtender, the CFO, nods. "I've had more than one person take me aside and ask what effect this will have on their annual reviews," he says. "They want to know if they're going to be judged on the number of services they come up with, and if a year goes by without one, does that mean they're going to be penalized for it? I think there are a lot of people who are privately upset that we've become a bit of a technology company. They just want to sell refrigerators and popcorn makers."

"That's exactly what I'm talking about—we could quickly lose focus of our core business if we're not careful here," Moneymaker says thoughtfully. "We've got aggressive growth targets to hit this quarter, and the last thing we need is everyone deciding this company is a playpen. Maybe we should formally explain what effect, if any, our innovation initiative will have on performance reviews— Frank," she looks to the CFO, "would you please look into that? And we need to let people know just what's expected from them in terms of dreaming up services. I've read that Google asks its employees to spend 20 percent of their time working on blue-sky ideas for the company, and 10 percent of their time working on whatever they want. Well, we're not Google, so maybe we should ask for 10 percent of some of our people's time instead of 30 percent."

Lovecraft can no longer restrain himself. "With all due respect, Jane," he says, "I think we're all being a little blind to the larger issues at stake here. The real risk isn't that our employees don't understand technology; it's that we're going to open ourselves up to viruses, hackers, industrial espionage, and even the risk of introducing wrong financial data into transactional systems that we can't explain away to the Feds when they realize we've violated Sarbanes-Oxley. I know you're a big believer in this Jane, but are you really prepared to go to jail if something goes horribly wrong?"

"Josh, you're being melodramatic."

"Not at all. It's hard enough for my team to keep tabs on individual users within this company when we're the ones handling installation and configuration. Giving them free run of this place would push us well past the breaking point. It is still far, far too early to hand them the keys to our enterprise applications via their homegrown services—we still don't have the policies, rules, and redundancies in place to secure ourselves against whatever malignancy their science projects drag in through the firewall. It's my job to make those guarantees, and I can't make them—I won't make them—while I'm busy trying to service-enable this company from the inside out."

At this point, David Firehammer, Vorpal's Chief Technical Officer, elects to speak up. "But Josh, for everything you just mentioned—viruses, hackers, whatever—we can build service-oriented solutions that are even more secure than what we have now. And you don't have to hook up the science projects to our production systems until your team's tested them. I know that the last thing I want is Vorpal employees or customers logging into our systems.

But that's the beauty of designing asynchronous services. If you want to be more secure, just build a user interface that handles the messaging, then require an audit trail through the service providers, and establish a contractual agreement arbitrated by a third party. It sounds to me like your team hasn't developed acceptable work flows or example architectures that are more secure by default. It's just a question of best practices—and not inside-out best practices, but outside-in best practices. I'm an advocate of keeping the corporate services shielded from the customer-facing services. We'll set up a buffer between them—think of it as a services-oriented DMZ."

"Maybe the solution here is to take this particular burden off your shoulders, Josh," Jane Moneymaker says. "Michael, are you willing to steer our efforts in that direction? Because, Josh, I need you to help me map out the way forward here. I know your concerns are legitimate, and no, I don't want to go to jail. But I also know that there is an equilibrium point between risk and reward in this strategy, and I think we're still erring a little in the direction of managing risk. Josh, Michael, we'll discuss this later, but we've got to come to some sort of consensus on this issue." Both men look at each other and nod.

"Good. Josh, I expect to see your thoughts on Mike's comments on the Intranet blog tomorrow. Now," she adds, "how are the mobile applications working out?"

"Oh, our people were already mobile," Lovecraft says. "We just weren't doing anything to help them until now. We've agreed that all new applications will be designed for an occasionally-connected model, which means our desktop and mobile users will get the same build and both benefit from the localized performance and reliability. We're starting to load these synchronizable applications onto laptops and even handhelds, and I've already noticed that my people aren't in the office as much. And it doesn't seem to be hurting their productivity, either. The only significant difference is the number of conference calls with kids making noise in the background, because everyone is working from home."

"That would explain my call with Lloyd Worrystein last week where, out of nowhere, he muffled the speaker and yelled 'I'M ON A CONFERENCE CALL WITH THE CEO'," Moneymaker laughs.

"On the other hand," the VP of marketing adds, "our 12-year-old son inadvertently listened in on an early morning strategy call last week with Europe and suggested a few ideas, one of which—the idea of seeding links to our mashups in mySpace—we're actually going to pursue."

From there, the conversation moves into a discussion of the company's online community activities. While building online communities has been embraced by employees, a few staffers have taken to them a little too enthusiastically, posting confidential material about upcoming products on an externally facing wiki vulnerable to prying eyes. Everyone agrees that some kind of management system needs to be put in place to control access and guide employees, while reinforcing the message with postings on the blog and eventually with training sessions.

"But what I'm most interested in," Moneymaker says, "are the suggestions for services. PopMe! started to scale—we went from 10, to hundreds, to thousands of channel partners—because we got the services right. So I'm very concerned we do the same internally. What do we have so far?"

"The most absurd was a suggestion for a vacation auto-approval service that rubber-stamped every request," says Lovecraft. "While it would have been good for morale, I think it would have severely affected productivity. In a close second place was the service that presented employees' salary information. Transparency is good... but only up to a point."

"What else have you got?"

"They seem to fall into three or four groups," he continues. "One is access to information. We've realized that our reporting infrastructure is inadequate in a couple of ways, and we think we can solve information bottlenecks with services.

"To give you just one example, we've already received a bunch of service requests for data we essentially already provide in spreadsheet form. But no one really knew about it, and no one was using it. As a first step to fix that, we've started advertising the fact that they can download the spreadsheets, but we've also crafted a few services that can deliver fresh data to any spreadsheet or application the user chooses. It's the difference between forcing them to use something, and maximizing their efficiency by giving them what they want in the form they want it. The early indications are that it's going to be a pretty popular service, and we're working on an external version of the same concept using Adobe Interactive Forms. Our initial discussions with our suppliers, channel partners, consultants, etc. indicated they are really going to like that."

"Let's get through the rest of the list; I only have another 10 minutes" Moneymaker says.

"About that list," Lovecraft replies, phrasing his words carefully. "I was hoping we could wait until after our scheduled ERP upgrade—which is still slated to take place in August—to implement the bulk of these. mySAP™ ERP 2005 has been practically rewritten from scratch to be completely service-enabled, and while we'd be sacrificing a few quarters, I think the long-term savings in developer hours and ease-of-use will more than make up for it."

"That's great," Moneymaker says, trying to stay calm, "but haven't we figured this out already? Don't we know which of the ideas on this list are the most important and need to be enabled more or less immediately?"

"Of course we do," Lovecraft replies soothingly, hoping to defuse the situation. "But if we wait just a bit longer, we'll have service-enabled the core of our business. I can't emphasize enough how much this will smooth the further development of services, and we won't have to worry about backward compatibility, buggy applications, and so on. The potential savings are immense."

Moneymaker takes a deep breath. Everyone around the table braces for a swift rebuke. "Look," she says, no longer trying to hide her frustration. "Haven't we learned the lesson of outside-in versus inside-out yet? We need to get these services to the people who need them and let our infrastructure play catch up. I don't believe that the costs we'll save will ever outweigh the opportunity cost of waiting six months—I think the negative impact of that delay is incalculable. How many times do I have to fight this battle? I'm not opposed to the upgrade—I understand why we need it, and why it will be worth it—but improving our system doesn't get the highest value stuff in the hands of our people or customers. "

Lovecraft suddenly looks struck dumb, realizing that he had slipped back into his old cost-cutting mindset. "Yeah, yeah, you're right," he mumbles. "There are actually a bunch of ways to support these, and there are many ways around the compatibility issues. In any case, we'll find a way to provide these services and more ASAP, but we still need some sort of published registry to keep track and publicize them…"

"Josh, I'll leave you to it," Moneymaker says, rising from her chair. "I'm late for my 10:30. I'll catch up with each of you this afternoon," she calls from the hallway.

■ Rules

As your company's service usage gradually increases, you will eventually hit a tipping point. While your services might begin life as powerful tools reserved for special projects and specific instances—like the original use for Vorpal's PopMe! application— sooner or later their proliferation within your company will mean that services have become an essential part of everyday work. When that moment arrives, maximizing the potential of your services will depend on retraining your employees to think about using them every day in every way—they can't remain the property of an elite few. The good news is that many of your employees have already created their own tools. The bad news is: they're hiding them from you.

Rule:
Promote Shadow IT

Understand that you have capabilities outside your IT department, and use them! Shadow IT is not new and exists in every company. It's been there, lurking just out of sight of your support teams, not necessarily hidden, but implemented by workers who need new tools, procedures, and workarounds that are not yet acknowledged by IT policies. They use their innovations every day to get their jobs and personal tasks done. With every class of graduating students, a more tech-literate labor force emerges. This labor force is creatively innovating both on and off the official clock. They bring with them new methodologies and models for working that line up directly with service orientation.

Trademark behaviors of the next generation building out Shadow IT solutions include the propensity to share everything, embracing the open source perspective, trying before buying, and utilizing a new generation of collaboration tools ranging from blogs, wiki's and social networking to embracing P2P technologies. Failure to embrace and support Shadow IT in the long run means wasted resources, an inability to maximize the value of your company's collective candlepower, and lost opportunities.

Rule:
Institute a Services Culture

Realize that innovation has become a constant activity, so learn how to enable it painlessly. Once you've succeeded in shedding some light on Shadow IT and encouraged your employees to begin building services, you'll need to have a process in place for the evaluation and propagation of their ideas. While you may not need to know about every employees' simple hacks that get them through the day, discovering a potential blockbuster idea like Hugo's original lightning strike shouldn't be left to chance.

Creating a lifecycle process, in which services are made, reported, judged, and finally supported by IT, is essential to maximizing the potential of your homegrown and ecosystem-developed services. While too much of anything is not necessarily a good thing, exercising care in selecting and standardizing reusable services can reap large benefits in both cost and labor savings. Tracking and promoting services reuse and corporate utilization of Shadow IT processes is proving to be lucrative.

Rule:
Realized Value Prioritizes Integration

Seize advantages with simple experiments before considering complex, full-scale integrated rollouts. As Vorpal learned from the PopMe! experience—when creating new services, perform the minimum amount of work to extract the value from a business opportunity, and start harvesting that value. Later, only after you've identified how the new services can be cost-optimized by interoperating with your hub IT services, take the steps necessary to integrate them. In some cases, maintaining less automated or manual processes may be the right answer for short-lived, or low volume, services. Make sure your edge technologies are effective before melding them with the hub, and don't wait for the hub to be ready before pursuing opportunities on the edges—they'll be long gone by then.

Rule:
Practice Safe SOA

Societies recognize the need for laws to protect freedoms; SOA enablement is no different. As with any emerging capabilities, the ability to establish robust, secure services is constantly evolving. "Safe SOA" refers to establishing methodologies, policies, and architectures that encourage the development and reuse of services that are "well behaved." This includes ensuring that services have appropriate legal disclaimers and licensing included, and that security and data quality measures are implemented. Safe SOA is also about developing robust services that continue functioning or gracefully terminate during network outages or in the absence of a mashed-up service. As new services are shared, a new level of application robustness emerges, as innovators' best ideas become best practices. For instance, sharing code that enables applications to test for the battery life available on a laptop or PDA will encourage all applications to check for battery status before engaging in an important action.

Reinforcing innovations ensures that the services your employees create stay within the bounds of acceptable usage. But for the company's own protection, assume that their creators either don't quite know what they're doing or possess malevolent intentions. Add security features, access controls, audit trails, and error recovery functionality to guarantee the scope and reliability of a service before it's released to general use.

Rule:
"End-to-End" is not the Beginning

Inability to show how a solution fits into the "end-to-end" business system has killed many an innovative idea. The term "end-to-end" has stood in for the nirvana the IT executives have consistently attempted to attain—the interconnection of every system across every business process, whether it's supply chains, manufacturing processes, or so on. Don't expect the services driving the hub IT systems to be in lockstep with your business innovations.

Do plan on continuously upgrading your hub infrastructure (inside-out) for generalized service enablement, but don't wait for that to happen before creating any services (outside-in). It may take awhile, for one thing, and if you begin building services in the meantime, your eventual upgrade will be faster and easier, as your developers will have developed the skill-sets necessary for doing so. Your company will be much better positioned to take full advantage of service-enabled platforms the moment they arrive.

Rule:
Mobility is not an Afterthought

The change to SOA also provides an opportunity to resolve the ongoing issue of retrofitting online systems and for mobility. Today, with the majority of users carrying cell phones and PDAs in addition to laptops or desktop systems, mobility has taken center stage. Because SOA services enable an asynchronous messaging architecture, the same characteristics that make services multi-lingual enable the design of new mobile architectures.

Starting from a "design for mobile" perspective means creating a single code base for applications instead of two—one for connected applications and one or more for mobile types. Applications built from the ground up, with mobility in mind, sport more reliable and responsive interfaces that can adapt to multiple devices.

They're inherently scalable and thus able to support a larger, increasingly mobile user base further down the road, and they're more reliable as a result of being tuned to run in the occasionally disconnected world of wireless devices. And, because mobile services enable the "point of work," businesses deploying mobile solutions are seeing significant improvements in productivity and revenue by mobilizing their business systems.

■ Putting the Rules to Work

It is in addressing the relationship between IT and the company that a program of SOA adoption becomes a cultural and program management issue that must be managed with care and forethought on a variety of dimensions.

The Generation Gap in IT

What we described above in this chapter as "Shadow IT" is actually the end result of 25 years of the PC's evolution. Everything we once lumped together under the heading of "productivity tools"—first the PC, followed a decade later by the Internet and then by ubiquitous wireless access a decade after that—has slowly morphed from the lowest spot on the IT totem pole into potentially potent tools. In the hands of a sophisticated user, these possess more than enough computing power and ease-of-use to act as de facto computing platforms, and hence the rise of Shadow IT.

It stands to reason then, that Shadow IT has not always existed. Part of the reason has to do with Moore's Law (that is, the technology was too weak and the infrastructure too incomplete until only recently), but the more important shift has been a demographic one. Shadow IT users overwhelmingly come from Generations X & Y, an age group that currently ranges from college graduates to an upper end of 45. Nearly all grew up with PCs; most have used the Internet since college, and their youngest cohorts now prefer text and instant messaging to the spoken word.

Collectively, they form the critical mass of users who grew up as computing natives and have the necessary sophistication for customizing their standard-issue IT into tools for optimizing their jobs and responsibilities. This is an unprecedented event in the short history of IT. Its first generation gap has emerged—users aged 45 and up, who expect IT to play its traditional role and cushion the effects of technology upon their everyday responsibilities, and those aged 35 and under, who expect to endlessly reshape IT in pursuit of the most efficient experience. The former group relies upon hub applications running smoothly, while the latter overwhelmingly comprise the edges, and are the originators of Shadow IT.

Going forward, companies will need to think long and hard about changing IT policies to reflect generational usage patterns. Providing some measure of flexibility may well become the norm, and the basic organization of business units may need to undergo wrenching change, as younger employees may need to step up to grasp opportunities offered by service-enablement, despite their lack of seasoning otherwise and the seniority issues this two-tiered model creates. Because this generation is both workers and consumers, the effects are two edged. Companies must not only support them in working in new ways but also must learn how to sell to them in the way they want to buy.

Creating a Program of Service Enablement

Before announcing to your company, à la Jane Moneymaker's email above, that the time has come to begin building services, rigorous research and planning is needed to determine the scope of your business opportunity, the service(s) needed to achieve it, and how those services fit within the larger context of your business.

It will be the extremely rare (and possibly foolhardy) company, other than a greenfield startup, that elects to service-enable its IT infrastructure from top to bottom all at once. As always, the safer and sounder approach is to start small, building individual services to meet business's immediate needs, then expand those into suites of services orchestrating business processes, before finally mapping your fully service-enabled to real world processes. The key is to build off successes at each level, creating services early on that can be easily incorporated into a more mature SOA that has been built following design patterns learned from building those early services.

Regardless of your approach, the process inevitably proceeds through three distinct stages before the first line of code is written: Discovery, when a business-driven analysis reveals the need for a service or services and requirements are drafted; Design, an iterative process in which the requirements are mapped onto services;

and Documentation, which involves properly documenting the new services for later in different constellations of services.

This process is commonly described as creating a program of service enablement, which can be as small or as large as your needs dictate. For our purposes, it would be easiest to describe such a program in terms of three levels, which are:

1. Designing a single service.
2. Designing systems of services.
3. Service-enabling your enterprise applications.

Level 1: Designing a Single Service

The need for a single service will most likely be spotted during the course of day-to-day business, where a gap in a business process or a missing piece of functionality might first inspire a shadow IT solution. A single, well-designed service can be a powerful, reusable tool—one that collects information spread across many systems and not only saves its creator a great deal of manual effort, but it can then be reused to perform similar tasks by multiple departments. Single services represent the lowest-hanging fruit for IT and solution designers, and an opportunity to hone skills in creating relatively simple services that will mesh easily with the complex systems to come.

Level 2: Designing Systems of Services

Once services addressing the gaps in the business processes have been created, the next iteration of service development is creating systems of services that support entire business processes. The available-to-promise (ATP) process step, for example, might be re-engineered as a collection of services that query internal systems across multiple factory and warehouse locations, suppliers' inventory systems, the inventory of work in progress, production schedules, etc. Your suppliers' systems, in turn, may use services to aggregate data from their own suppliers, as your request cascades down the supply chain.

Representing this ballet of data requests in service form will likely require a combination of existing services which can be reused (assuming they were designed correctly) and others that must be built. Unlike designing a single service, in which the only task at hand is addressing a glaring need, creating systems of services demands balancing the requirements of the process in question with the maximal usefulness of the services being created to address that process (since they will ultimately be reused in the name of the greater good). In practice, that could easily mean redesigning the business process itself to glean the maximum benefit from the design efforts.

The key to creating a useful set of services—which becomes especially clear in the next level—that will both work together to support its business process, and be reused separately as many times as possible to support others as well. Bad service design is building services and business objects that aren't sufficiently granular to allow for easy reuse; good design is decomposing process steps into a suite of services that can then be orchestrated to solve the business need in question, while allowing for recombination. Designers must also be on the lookout for patterns that appear during the course of development—service orchestrations, interface designers, common elements of any type—as they will prove to be a great aid upon reaching the final level.

Level 3: Service-enabling Your Enterprise Applications

Once your company understands how services work on their own and in concert to automate business processes, it's time to begin a more comprehensive program of service enablement. The technical goal is the eventual transformation of your enterprise application into galaxies of services, thus increasing their flexibility, integration, and so on. But, as we have maintained throughout this book, it's almost pointless to transform your IT infrastructure if the business fails to benefit from it. The greater goal, and challenge, is to undertake a large-scale analysis of every business process and systematically transform the underlying IT into services.

It's an enormous challenge, and so far to date, no company is that far along in its evolution to an SOA. But as organizations slowly accrete experience and a foundation of services from their early efforts, the speed of adoption should accelerate as design patterns and modeling tools assist in the rapid creation and modification of composite applications.

Any company can begin crafting a program of service enablement, although the first companies to do so in earnest are software makers and the very largest organizations (with the largest IT budgets to match).

Rethinking Your Architecture

The ultimate implications of total service enablement go far beyond optimizing your existing business processes and inventing new applications. Fully realized SOAs offer the opportunities to rethink the structure of the company itself and to re-imagine how your business activities really contribute value to your customers' lives. They offer the chance to reconstruct the physical structure of the firm—hierarchies, departments, and siloed applications—in the image of the process flows that actually define it.

The physical structure of the firm as we know it is actually the result of the inherent limitations of creating, sorting, and storing data in a pre-digital, pre-networked era. Attempts to grapple with the growing complexity of corporations in the 19th century led to physical centralization (office towers and factory floors) and inevitably to the filing cabinet, the Victorian Era's database. The limitations of the filing cabinet were a metaphor for the increasing inability of firms to keep a firm grasp on end-to-end business processes. As companies continued growing in size and scope, divisions and subdivisions (into departments, and sub-departments) were necessary to impose any kind of order on day-to-day activities. To paraphrase the biologist Sir D'Arcy Wentworth Thompson: growth creates form, but form limits growth. The form of the modern corporation was created by constraints that, within an SOA, suddenly cease to exist.

The challenge in the SOA era will be to reshape the physical structure of the firm to mirror the actual flow processes underneath. Why? Because the current structure contributes as many obstacles and inefficiencies to business processes as it does strengths. Consider a retail bank that cannot offer its customers a single picture of their finances, because their data is being scattered across half a dozen databases in an equal number of departments that were set in stone more than a century ago. But many banks have already begun to undo this, merging data into a single flow process that allows their customers to blur the boundaries between checking accounts, credit cards, mortgages, and so on.

The point is: do not undertake the Herculean task of service-enabling your organization without being prepared to imagine what you could look like when you're finished. Building an SOA is only the first step.

■ Examples

Much of the effort that has gone into implementing an SOA focuses on the creation of services to expose as much functionality as possible. But the payoff must wait until somehow the services are put into action. These two examples illustrate the return from simple support for mobility and from a powerful tool for taking advantage of a general suite of services.

Snap-on's Mobile Solution

Simple yet effective mobile solutions can have a massive impact. Snap-on tools, a global leader in professional tools, diagnostics, and equipment, is a familiar brand to anyone who loves cars and spends time in auto repair garages. The company's products are sold through a network of approximately 3,500 franchisees who use trucks emblazoned with the Snap-on logo as mobile stores and visit customers in their routes.

A majority of the time, Snap-on products are sold from inventory carried on the trucks, but sometimes the franchisees need to call one of Snap-on's four distribution centers to check on product availability. For many franchisees, this took place 4 to 6 times a day, with calls typically ranging from 5 to 15 minutes each.

To speed up the product availability checks and to distribute the latest information to each franchisee, Snap-on crafted a mobile solution called the Mobile Information Center, which utilizes Intellisync Mobile Suite software from Nokia to synchronize information. Many Snap-on trucks are equipped with a laptop with Wi-Fi and/or WWAN capability. Whenever the laptops are connected to the network (which may be while at a client site, in an office, or via a home-network) the latest changes to the Mobile Information Center are automatically synchronized to their laptops. Instead of calling Snap-on to check product availability, they can use the Mobile Information Center to immediately view the latest synchronized inventory information from each of the four distribution centers. The latest product information is also synchronized to the laptops.

The franchisees love the solution because it saves them about 3 or more hours a week by speeding inventory checking. Each hour saved translates into roughly three more customer interactions. The results? All franchisees in the pilot group that have implemented the Mobile Information Center have exceeded the national average for sales.

Enterprise Horizons

Services create the opportunity to extend existing hub systems with a new breed of technology enabling creative use of the information available from core business systems. Companies like Enterprise Horizons are providing tools and plumbing to amplify the value of service-enabling an enterprise. The four-year old company provides a framework for combining geographic information and overlaying thematic business-related information on top so that the data and the visualization are combined in ways that encourage deeper understanding and new insights. For instance, linking a Google Maps User experience to SAP's CRM solution via SAP's Netweaver platform is allowing Enterprise Horizon's customers to visualize information previously trapped in reports or dashboards.

Imagine visualizing the experience of driving by your billboard ad placement prior to purchasing it while visualizing real physical and business demographic information associated with the specific billboard location. Enterprise Horizon's Multi-function Adaptation of Geoinformative Mashups (MAGMA) Ecosystem creates stunning graphic worlds in which traditional bar and pie charts leap out of satellite imagery, providing insight into clustering or patterns that would be hard to see otherwise.

The emergence of platforms like the MAGMA Ecosystem increases the payoff for opening up hub systems through services. Much of the action in the early development of SOA platforms has focused on the tools needed to create services and efforts to create libraries of services based on transactional hub systems. With SOA solutions now emerging, the focus becomes putting those services to work to gain competitive advantage.

Chapter 6

Internal IT

For the past six months, the organizational changes wrought by services have crashed over Vorpal like a tidal wave. First they washed over the edges, where they transformed the relationships between innovators, customers and the company, and now they're finally breaking over the core. How will the structure and responsibilities of the IT department itself be affected by services? How will it manage to support both the stable processes of the hub and rapid developments on the edges?

These questions had been staring Josh Lovecraft and his team in the face since Jane Moneymaker's call to arms at the beginning of the year. That had unleashed a second flood on the IT department, which now found itself swamped with three competing duties: tending to Vorpal's core business systems, just as they always had; racing to finish their current checklist of development projects; and doing their best to support the new grassroots efforts of employees, suppliers, sales channels and customers assembling their own DIY IT on the edges. After barely a month, the team is exhausted and cracks in the department's current structure have become all too obvious.

With the end of March approaching, Lovecraft decides to use his quarterly meeting as the forum for hashing out a new structure capable of coping with its new responsibilities...

Adapting the Shape of IT

"Hi everyone," Josh opens the meeting. "It's been an exhilarating and an exhausting three months, and considering that I can't even keep track of what I'm supposed to be doing," the room laughs nervously, "I have to confess that I haven't kept up as much as I'd like with some of you, either. I'd like to start this meeting with everyone telling me what they're working on, and what we need to work on to be better as a whole."

"Frankly, Josh, I think we're all a bit confused about who does what anymore," offers his VP of engineering.

"Yeah," says the VP of ERP. "While I'm really excited about where our edge initiatives are going—some days I feel like we're working at a Silicon Valley startup, because having ideas and implementing them quickly is what my guys live for—the problem is that everyone, and I mean everyone thinks they have a great idea, and everyone wants to work on it. And when a problem comes up, as they inevitably do, no one knows who's going to take care of it."

"My job has changed from one where I kept the core systems of this company running to one where I'm desperately trying to support rank and file employees who are suddenly pushing the performance of their machines and their tools to the limit," the Director of End-User Support chimes in. "We've had to change all of our day-to-day support policies, and not for the better—we have to explain all the time that there are limits on the amount of help we can give them, and so a lot of these "great ideas" are just dying on the vine before we ever know whether that's a good thing or a bad thing."

As the conversation winds its way around the conference table, it becomes crystal clear that everyone in IT is struggling to support the service-enabled company Vorpal has become. "People have been creating lots and lots of services—and departmental managers tell us that productivity is up—but they need a lot of help in figuring out how to actually use them," the Director of Development adds. "They know they want the information that services can provide, but when it comes time to compose those services into a functional application, the Peter Principle kicks in in earnest, and that's when they suddenly need our help. They can play with a spreadsheet all day, but they can't compose an application to save their lives, to tell you the truth. I'm now coercing people into reusing the more generic services we've built, because they're already robust and it's saving a lot of time."

Lovecraft takes all of this in, and when his managers have finished venting, he pushes back his chair and stands at the head of the table. "We were originally organized to serve the needs of our company's core business systems (hub). But that's changed, obviously, with our having to support the new business being generated at the fringes of our company. But I think the key to supporting both is to realize what the hub systems and the edge systems are actually *doing*.

"Before SOA, we were using our edge web sites to talk to customers, help them, find new ones—all of this stuff *interactional* and *informational*," he says, walking over to the whiteboard in the corner and writing those under the heading "EDGE". "Adding services is making the edge Transactional, too. It's like we have two set's of core business systems, the ones connecting our business to the world and the ones keeping our business running.

"But our hub systems have to be rock solid for security and compliance concerns. Jane may love her golden boys down in marketing, but I doubt even she's ready to go to jail if Hugo Wunderkind and his merry band turn out to be a bunch of crooks. If the moment any of our customers completes a transaction it's automatically handed off to the ERP system in the hub we could be setting ourselves up for disaster. While edge services can and should be experimental, wide-ranging, homegrown, etc., our even larger task is to ensure the validity and sanctity of our core data. And that means securing those spokes linking the edges to the hub. Dave Firehammer was right about needing a Services DMZ. Using the spoke systems to validate, filter and ensure data quality prior to submitting the transactions into the core business systems of the hub is now on the critical path.

"That's one thing we have to keep in mind. The other is where all of our service-enablement efforts are headed for the hub systems themselves. We're still due to upgrade to mySAP ERP 2005 in the third quarter, and SAP has promised us that the latest version will ship with their 'Enterprise Service Repository,' and that all future versions of their flagship application will more or less be rewritten as services. So it's safe to say that in a few years, this entire company will be running on services, not just the tinkering that's currently going on at the fringes.

"And finally we may have a chance to wrap our minds around the whole problem here," says Firehammer, the CTO. "For as long as I've been in IT, we've been looking for an architecture that could actually support the entire business from end to end. And now we have a pretty good view of what the end-to-end business looks like. We have the edges full of loose interaction surrounding a locked down transactional hub. For me, the huge sigh of relief is that SOA is an architecture that supports both. Services can be provided into the looser context and we can reach in and expose just what we need from the hub."

"You're right," says Lovecraft, "and the unifying theme is process. SOA can support the informal processes at the edge and the more formal controlled processes at the hub. But our organization is not focused on the processes that flow through the business and how SOA supports them, and that's the problem.

"So here's my thinking," Lovecraft says, as he hastily begins scribbling on the whiteboard. "This company is currently organized by departments, of which IT is one, and within each department are sub-departments, and so on. Our hub applications have, until now, been written and designed to reflect the same hierarchy.

"Now, virtually nothing this company does is contained within one department. The official org chart is beginning to matter less and less around here, and our drive to support services on the edge is only accelerating that. So... with all of that in mind, I think it's time to practice what we preach here in IT. Our structure has to support the company we're becoming, if that makes any sense.

"Now, let's be good citizens about this—I know that anytime I bring up changes to the org chart, people start fretting about their turf—but let's just try to put those concerns aside for a little while and try to figure out what could be the right organization for us in this services era we're in. Here's where we're at now:

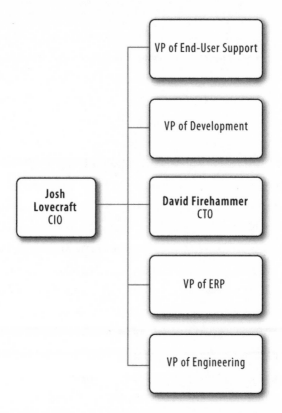

"So looking from the outside-in, what are our current responsibilities, in fact, if not in name? The first one is to the edge. That being whatever services and productivity tools we have at our disposal to further the aims of the business. Some people are doing this for themselves, which leads them to suggest services, which results in... what? New services, new ideas for desktop tools, and eventually new applications when the few people who know what they're doing put something together. So what do we have when we combine all of these? People who are innovating—people who are stirring the pot. What do we call those? I like 'disruptive innovators,' so we'll call them that for now.

"Okay, so then—they're bubbling with ideas for services, they're creating the services themselves. Our responsibility to them is to facilitate their innovation. But we have to protect this from becoming a mess. We have to provide tools and create reusable services for them (In Web 2.0 terms APIs) and then what?"

The VP of development chimes in, "and then we're stuck molding them into applications, which is where the trouble starts, as most people don't know what to do with them. We really need people who are close to their own lines of business who can be trusted to compose applications. So what we have then are people combining and recombining services in pretty much the same way as what the marketing boys have done with mashups."

"You're absolutely right," Lovecraft says. "That's our second group. We'll call them 'composers.' They're managers or superusers who know what the hell they're doing in terms of creating applications. They're the ones who are actually restructuring this company, process by process, and they're becoming the spokes connecting the edge to the hub guaranteeing the sanctity of the data that's passed to our core systems."

"But they need guidance," says Firehammer. "They know the micro-process that they are working on, but without help, they won't see the macro picture. That has to be someone's job, and it is vast and important."

"Well, its your job now," Lovecraft says. "I dub thee our first acting Chief Process Officer. I'll check with Jane to see if this will fly as a title, but the need for the position is clear, and it is a full-time job. I'm not sure one that you want in the long term. We have to have someone shaping and influencing the grass roots composition efforts within a larger process architecture that makes sense. But that raises another question, which is: Who's keeping track of services for supporting the processes?

"I mean, we have three or four vendors delivering service repositories to us besides SAP, and we're not using every service in any of them. And then we have all of our homegrown services as well, and we're having trouble keeping track of those and explaining what's in our central repository at any given moment. So we need someone keeping track of a master repository."

"Are those the same people composing applications?" the VP of engineering asks. "Because I don't think they should be; that should be left to the pros, otherwise our data quality is suspect. We should recognize services design for the object-oriented analysis task that it is. When we expose a service from the hub, we have to do so carefully and protect ourselves."

"Agreed," Lovecraft replies. "I think that's still another group, the repository keepers," adding yet another heading to the whiteboard. "They're the ones responsible for developing and enforcing policies that ensure data integrity, security, and other compliance issues are met."

"Josh, now that we're finishing off our last set of core projects, almost everything on our to-do list for this fiscal year is service-related. Like you said, software development at this company has become building services and service enablement. So what about all the consolidation we have planned?" asks the VP of ERP.

"Yep, we're still doing that," Lovecraft says adding a consolidator box to his diagram. "In fact, we are still doing everything we are doing now. Frank Cashtender, the CFO, is still going to be pressing me to squeeze out costs and rationalize the systems at the hub, you can be sure of that."

"And considering how large this company is, we'll never stop consolidating," concurs the VP of ERP. "And even if we did somehow finish wringing every last cost out of the environment, Jane would just buy another company, and we'd have to start all over again."

"There's your structure right there, ladies and gentlemen," Lovecraft says, gesturing toward the headings he's scribbled on the whiteboard. "We have 'disruptive innovators' driving the edge, 'repository keepers' and 'consolidators' tending to our hub systems, 'composers' who are creating the linkages between the two along lines of business processes and not just department structure, and there you go. So let's write that down and figure out how to do this."

"But what about communicating the big picture?" the VP of ERP asks. "Who's worried about that besides me? We understand this new structure but to work effectively the rest of the business will have to know what we are up to and know their appropriate role. That's what we are struggling with now. There's lots of energy in the company, but some of it is unfocused and misdirected. When the buzz of Hugo's victory dies down, people must understand how the new focus is on defining processes and supporting them with SOA."

"We're all responsible for driving toward service-oriented architectures and educating those who we work with," Lovecraft says, "because I think we're dealing with three distinct functions that must work together. We have the hub, the edges and the services and processes unify them. The hub is everything we've been doing all along—running stable enterprise systems, etc., except now the hub will be comprised of services. Composing common services for business process reuse provides us with layers of reliability and compliance while we provide services and tools to the edges to accelerate innovation and business results."

"But it's trickier than that," the Director of End-user Support interjects. "We can't just show up in people's departments and tell them, 'here are a bunch of tools and services.' We've told them that all along, and it hasn't done much good, apparently. If they need tools to build their own services, yada yada yada, then they need to tell us what it is, exactly, that they need. We need at least one person in each product group, or whatever, who can tell us that."

"Done," Lovecraft says. "We'll find those people. We have to staff the educational process. Let's call them 'Edge Liaisons' or whatever. We'll put someone in charge of figuring those things out, and I'm sure that in every case they won't be older than 25." The room chuckles.

A New Org Chart for a New Era of IT

The week after the meeting, a draft for a new organizational chart emerges from the printer in Josh Lovecraft's department. It looks something like this:

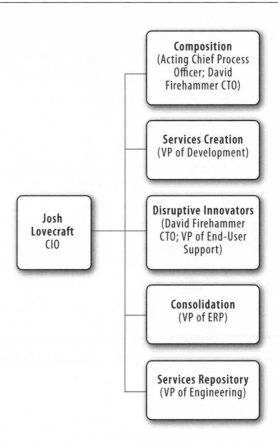

■ Rules

As service enablement sweeps through the company, its wide-spread adoption will inevitably stretch the resources of IT to the limit. Having been designed to serve the hub functionality of the company, IT departments will respond to service adoption as best they can, but their structure won't permit them to support efforts at the edges to maximize business advantages. Clearly, a change in approach is needed, not only in terms of structure, but also in development methodology. Competitive business advantage dictates that IT's struggles with massive development or consolidation projects that were spec'd out years ago cannot continue.

Rule:
Reorganize Around Service Delivery

Replace the big project mentality of IT with a build-and-run-fast culture. Until now, the organizing principle of IT has been the care and feeding of the monolithic enterprise applications that comprise hub systems. The staggering complexity and power of these applications ensured that only experts would ever be able to access or alter them, which in turn guaranteed that IT would be left alone in tending, installing, upgrading and retiring them.

But just as service delivery promises to be a new model for IT, supporting it demands a new organizational structure for IT departments. They are being forced to support the hub *and* the edges in equal measure, which today's org charts are ill equipped to do. How can the departmental focus give way to a business or process focus? And what then, is the correct model?

SAP executive Shai Agassi has offered a structure which Vorpal's new org chart (shown above) is drawn from. In the service-enabled future SAP sees dawning, Agassi recommends that IT departments refocus around a number of crucial areas. Two of these incorporate individuals who have not traditionally worked within IT.

The first such group is the "disruptive innovators," those who sit on the bleeding edges, so to speak. They are the ones constantly scouting for new opportunities in their respective lines of business, and thus are continually spitting out ideas for new tools, new applications, new everything. This IT unit is designed to support the brainstormers.

The other group includes the "application composers," who are essentially line managers armed with the tools and sufficient training to confidently assemble services into lightweight applications. (Of course, the composition of larger scale applications will still be the province of IT.)

By relinquishing the initiative to create these tools and applications to line-of-business employees rather than insisting on building everything itself, IT is able to support both the hub and the edge without either a huge infusion of resources or the possibility of a meltdown.

Former hub functions are then subdivided into three new areas as well: a service development team, in charge of creating new services to support and further business aims; repository keepers in charge of administering the company's growing arsenal of services arriving from vendors, the service development team, and homegrown efforts by employees; and finally, the consolidation team, which continues to look for opportunities to reduce costs in stable systems.

Although this is just one suggested structure, it's imperative that IT reconsider its current division of duties in order to support the grassroots efforts of individuals working on the edges of the company.

Rule:
Optimize Service Development

Good enough, rather than perfect, is the target when systems are not being built to last. Just as IT is currently designed to administer fantastically complex enterprise applications, today's development methodologies are similarly complex, inflexible, and guaranteed to last for years, if not decades.

Web 2.0 solutions are often said to be in "constant beta." Adapting to a service-enabled world where the constructions of services and applications are radically simpler and faster requires retiring the classic approach of elaborately mapping specifications on a whiteboard and then spending two years hand-coding them.

Instead of plotting to build virtual cathedrals, the application and service development team must embrace new, more agile approaches to creating reusable code that is battle-tested in everyday life, refined, and then tested again. An iterative approach would simultaneously guarantee that products reach the hands of users in record times, and produce usage insights that could be harvested for further improvements during the next development cycle.

■ Putting the Rules to Work

Agile Development Methods

The inherent flexibility of services—their ability to encapsulate functionality and recombine it as needed—won't do much good in building applications unless the current practices for building them change to reflect these new capabilities. While the typical 9- to 18-month development cycle may shrink thanks to productivity gains gleaned from using services, you won't really gain the ability to rapidly adapt to changing business conditions until your development methodology is specifically designed to support them.

In practice, this means shifting the focus from the hub to the edge—from the general-purpose infrastructure focused on cost reduction, to the ability to support many more business processes in micro-environments focused on supporting new lines of business and capturing revenue. Instead of building applications which you hope will last in the same form for years, you should work toward building the right architecture that allows the application to change affordably ten times within the same period, as it's continually recast to meet changing business conditions. Doing so correctly requires an architecture that allows you to move toward your business objectives in smaller increments.

Adopting agile development methods is a first step toward unlocking the full potential of services and achieving the business impact they promise. They replace the classical "waterfall" methods—in which one step inextricably leads down to the next, with no going back—with a more iterative approach. The former follows what is essentially a five-step method:

- Create the requirements
- Design the system
- Implement it
- Debug it
- Launch it

The problem is that systems designed this way fail quite often because the initial requirements were either poorly defined at the beginning, or because they had changed during development owing to shifting business conditions.

The only way to address this fundamental flaw, according to agile development proponents, is to take a humble view of your ability to accurately gather requirements. Instead of pretending you can determine the requirements of a large solution, focus on smaller pieces of functionality. You can implement those pieces in iterations of short duration, and then put them into production.

Using these smaller components, you confirm your understanding of the true requirements users have in the field. All throughout, you're building confidence in your ability to take the next step forward, which builds upon what you've accomplished already.

In this way, agile development replaces the vicious circles of traditional development with a feedback loop that allows for end users to provide insights into what the proper next steps and requirements should be. Thus, large systems are built from small steps.

These approaches intrinsically take advantage of services and business process modeling, rather than ignoring their potential in the development process. Three of these approaches will be discussed here: eXtreme Programming, Scrum, and the Rational Unified Process.

eXtreme Programming

eXtreme Programming attempts to shrink the development process to a very tight loop, and creates software that is built to be changed and improved. Requirements are expressed as "stories"—simple explanations of what users wanted from the system—and one of its ironclad rules is to never implement imagined future requirements, only what's needed right now. Iterations take place within a defined period, and the scope of what can be accomplished may change instead of compromising the quality of the software produced. eXtreme Progamming's observation is that in most projects, of all the constraints on a project—scope, time, resources, and quality—quality is usually the one that suffers.

Another core tenet of eXtreme Programming is its "test-first" methodology, which means that even before features are implemented, tests are created to confirm that the eventual functionality will work properly. The test-first approach guarantees that at the end of the first programming cycle, a definitive means for testing the code and ensuring it works properly is in place. It also alleviates the fear that changing any portion of the code base might lead to unforeseen disruptions at runtime—thanks to the rigorous testing mechanisms, potential disruptions can be easily traced. Other practices in eXtreme Programming include programming in pairs, common ownership of code, and keeping the users and the programmers in the same room during development.

The net result is a greater degree of engineering quality and confidence—practitioners feel free to iterate and rebuild projects as often as necessary, with little chance of inadvertently breaking their code.

Scrum

Scrum was developed as a response to frequent failures in project management and communication, specifically a failure to create a firm set of project requirements and resist the temptation to add to them or constantly change your mind. Chronic indecision can be just as deadly to a project as unrealistic requirements.

Scrum addresses this by replacing the traditional project management model with a new approach in which managers on the business side create a list of requirements achievable in the next increment of development, and then sort these requirements from highest priority to lowest. The development team commits to a strict time limit and a specific subset of the highest priority requirements. (A month is a typical amount of time in Scrum projects.)

In daily planning meetings called "scrums," each member of the development team presents what they accomplished yesterday, what they intend to do today, and what obstacles lie in their path. The "Scrum Master's" job is to remove those obstacles, leaving the self-organizing development team to race to complete their goals within the strict time limit allotted to them. And once the scope of a scrum is set, it cannot be changed by anyone, short of ending the scrum prematurely.

All of this amounts to shock therapy for development teams prone to changing requirements and adding features on the fly until projects are brought to a standstill by indecision. No matter what else happens, Scrum promises that some discrete quantity of development work will be finished at the end, which is no small accomplishment.

The Rational Unified Process

The Rational Unified Process is a methodology for large-scale system development in which incremental development is used to confirm an emerging understanding of a highly complex system. Projects using this method start with an "inception phase," in which the vision, business case, and scope are mapped out, along with a vague estimate of how long development will take. This is followed by an "elaboration phase" in which the vision is refined, iterative development focused on the core architecture and high risk elements is performed, and, based on this experience, more detailed requirements and scope are created. In the "construction phase," iterative development of the lower risk and easy elements is done, as well as preparations for deployment. And the "transition phase" contains testing and deployment.

The Rational Unified Process attempts to organize the design work necessary for a large system into a sequence of steps that use iterative development to confirm the accuracy of requirements. Its practitioners are able to grapple with the massive complexity of large-scale projects on the one hand, while continually adjusting and confirming requirements on the other.

Which One is Right for You?

The answer is: it depends. eXtreme Programming can help you address problems of engineering quality and will also create systems that can be changed with confidence; it's aimed squarely at developers writing code. Scrum is a way to force focus in an organization so that everyone can agree on what is to be done in the next increment. And Rational Unified Process is a road map for conquering the complexity of large systems. eXtreme Programming and Scrum can even be used in combination in instances where code quality is suffering *and* the relationship between the business side and IT is more or less broken. The former helps rebuild confidence in the quality of the product while the latter is an attempt to mend that relationship and balance the power dynamics between the two sides. The Rational Unified Process is an even more ambitious attempt to maintain the central role of system designers while acknowledging the difficulty of gathering accurate requirements, then using iterative development methods to confirm them along the way.

In the end, it matters less which of these methodologies (or any others) you choose, than using this knowledge to work through the changes in IT organization, attitude and skill sets that will put SOA to work in your business as quickly and as frequently as possible.

The Politics of SOA

Before your CIO can busy him- or herself with transforming your organization from the inside-out and outside-in via service enablement, he or she will first have to restructure the IT department itself to support that task, which makes IT the front line in the political battles that will no doubt be waged as a result of the evolution toward using SOA to business advantage.

Some will not go quietly; in fact, they will moan, complain, bicker and fret during the transition from a traditional IT staff to one capable of supporting SOA. It's beyond the scope of this book to offer a comprehensive survival guide, but suffice it to say that the scene at Vorpal described above was an exceptionally smooth changeover.

Perhaps the best way to imagine the transition is to imagine a spreadsheet with each IT executive owning a vertical column filled with his or her own responsibilities, which in turn represents pieces of the horizontally-oriented processes that flow across their various domains. The goal is to ultimately rearrange this imaginary spreadsheet so that each of the deputies in question gradually move from the vertical to the horizontal and assume the responsibility of an internal IT process—such as repository keeping, or leading the disruptive innovators, etc.

In the beginning, there will be resistance, especially by senior staffers who have grown competent and comfortable enough in their roles. It will be the younger, more ambitious employees (the Hugo Wunderkinds of IT) who lead the charge and pick up the reins of early service-enablement projects. But once those have begun to take root in the company, and after processes that span ERP, CRM, and other enterprise applications have drawn the employees who tend to them into an SOA, the overwhelming logic of redesigning applications around business process flows gradually breaks down resistance.

Winning the political battles surrounding an SOA isn't achieved by fiat anymore than building an SOA is achieved by breaking every application down into services all at once and declaring it finished. Just as the advantages of enabling services accumulate over time, so does the inherent sense of realigning IT to support it. In the end, you won't need to convince your IT team of the rightness of implementing SOA; they will already be surrounded by an ecosystem of innovators drawing them in.

■ Examples

While companies are generally reticent to discuss internal processes, the importance of well-managed IT has caused many more companies to open the kimono about their IT management strategy. The sharing of best practices is the CIO equivalent of sharing services in Web 2.0 and SOA environments. In charting its evolution to SOA, Intel is both tracking its own progress and seeking to define the optimal balance in its approach to IT architecture.

Enterprise Architecture @ Intel Corporation

Intel Corporation is making a broad transition in its approach to enterprise architecture that demonstrates how SOA will be adopted by the largest organizations. The company is moving at a steady pace from a historical emphasis on business domain silos to a solution-focused approach supported by competencies in business, data, applications, and technology. Ultimately, Intel's solution focus will result in a fully realized service-oriented enterprise.

Intel analyzes its IT infrastructure in terms of core systems that provided differentiating value and commodity systems that support the context for the business. As much as possible, IT resources are aligned to focus on core solutions that provide the highest corporate return while commodity solutions and outsourcing drive down the cost of non-differentiating functionality.

The design and continued evolution of Intel's IT infrastructure is governed by a formal enterprise architecture process that was launched in 2003 and has taken increasing advantage of SOA to promote reuse of standard functionality. According to Gregg Wyant, Chief Architect at Intel, the 2006 organizational goals at Intel to manage their transition to services is recognizably similar to the structure proposed by Vorpal including:

- Business and Data Architecture teams who partner and align to propel the company to business model driven development
- New Solution Architecture teams who create a single point of accountability and decision making, and decrease time-to-solution
- Services Creation teams and Forward Engineering who work together to drive rapid adoption and implementation of SOA
- Consolidation team that focuses on continuous improvement of services and capabilities
- Operations and Strategic Vendor Management team to keep architecture on track

At Intel, as with many large enterprises, establishing value metrics is crucial to gaining executive level support. In 2003 the architecture team negotiated tangible metrics for the CFO associated with service reuse. They set out creating a culture of reuse including a site for sharing and educating developers on the services available for reuse. The cumulative cost savings since 2003 is now well over $100 million. Equally impressive is the human factor, with an estimated 1 million person hours saved in 2005.

Application of SOA must be carefully targeted to be effective. Wyant's team estimates that after the cost of developing and maintaining services for reuse, it takes approximately 2.5 implementations of a service to recoup the investment. By the 3rd use of a service in a business process, the organization is saving time and money.

The ultimate goal for Intel's IT infrastructure is to create a comprehensive fabric for a service-oriented enterprise in which applications services, platform services, and infrastructure services all work in harmony to meet business needs. To meet this challenge, companies like Intel must address fundamental infrastructure issues that are not explored in detail in this book. While IT and Business architects, and software companies supporting them, are evolving toward SOA, an equally fundamental hardware ecosystem must be created. This Service-Oriented Infrastructure (SOI) becomes the building blocks on which SOA can thrive. An SOI takes advantage of advances in computing technology to provide utilities of computing, network and storage resources. In the future, it is likely that such resources, either virtualized or not, will be orchestrated to provide an optimal platform for the next generation of services.

Chapter 7

Our Story Ends, Yours Begins

The Daily Snark

September 10, 2007

Hed: Popping a New Business

Dek: Vorpal Builds a Channel from the Outside-In

MORRIS PLAINS, N.J.—Hugo Wunderkind had just finished making a fresh batch of popcorn on a Sunday afternoon last football season when his 5-year-old daughter Emily began scribbling on the popper with a Magic Marker. Mr. Wunderkind, 28, was then a marketing manager at Vorpal Inc., the kitchen appliance subsidiary of Jabberwocky Co. that manufactured the Pop-Matic popcorn popper in his living room that afternoon, where family and friends had ritually gathered to watch their beloved New York Jets.

Hugo Wunderkind

As Emily drew the uniform and number of her favorite player, wide receiver Laveranues Coles, on the side of the popcorn maker, Mr. Wunderkind had an inspiration. "Why not sell Pop-Matics to Jets fans with the logo already on the popper?" he recalls wondering that afternoon. "Or why not offer any fan the opportunity to stick an image on the side?"

But rather than pitch the idea to his superiors, he recruited a friend and coworker to assist him in building a web application that could render images on Pop-Matics, such as a photo of Mr. Coles taken from the Jets' web site. Then Mr. Wunderkind posted the finished application, which he today describes as "a toy" on his personal web log.

Vorpal hasn't been the same company since.

Mr. Wunderkind's toy touched off what his boss, Vorpal CEO Jane Moneymaker, unabashedly describes as a "revolution" at Vorpal, one that created more than two dozen new products, led to exclusive deals with the National Football League and Major League Baseball, and eventually led to radical restructuring of the company's supplier relationships and own departments.

"We've come to realize that our customers aren't necessarily as interested in purchasing a popcorn popper or a grill," Ms. Moneymaker says, "as they are in creating a communal experience. They want to share our great communal moments—watching a game or a match with their friends and family—and we're reinventing our products to reflect that. We'll be a different company in a few years."

Jane Moneymaker

The result is that a once-staid division of Jabberwocky is poised to post a double-digit percentage increase in revenue this year for the first time in more than a decade. Vorpal's revenues in the first six months of this year rose 12%, to $292.5 million.

And last week, Jabberwocky CEO and chairman Chuck Dodgson announced in an internal memo that other company units, including its March Hare superstores and Cheshire Technologies, would also begin to adopt the experimental technologies that have driven the change at Vorpal. "I think this company has a lot to learn from what Jane's done at Vorpal," Dodgson told The Daily Snark in an interview. "She really went down the rabbit hole, and we're poised to follow her."

The technologies in question are a more advanced form of web services, an arcane term for methods to make software components automatically work together over the Internet. Software industry heavyweights Microsoft, Oracle, SAP, and IBM have all launched major efforts in recent years to establish themselves as the standard bearers of the shift to web services. Microsoft was first when it unveiled its .NET initiative back in 2000, while services are at the heart of SAP's plan to achieve its audacious goal of more than tripling its customer base to around 100,000 by 2010. Customers of all four giants and many of their smaller competitors have warily embraced services so far, preferring to wait and see what mature offerings will look like.

Vorpal is the exception in that the overwhelming majority of its services were homegrown, developed internally by its own programmers and deployed in the service of its burgeoning customized appliance business, the driver behind its newfound growth. Ms. Moneymaker's decision to rely less and less on the classical information technology model of "best of breed" applications supplied by different vendors and choosing to pursue services-powered integration led to sweeping changes across the company.

"We're an undeniably more transparent, more fluid, more empowering, and more responsive company than we were 12 months ago," Ms. Moneymaker says, "all because we let our customers, suppliers, and partners tell us how we could best serve them, or have them best serve us, and how to let them serve themselves in the process."

They Will Come and Help Build It

Mr. Wunderkind was shocked last fall when a visitor to his blog tried to order a custom Pop-Matic using the toy application he had built. "I couldn't believe it; he even provided a credit card number and shipping address," says Mr. Wunderkind, who is now a director in charge of Vorpal's online marketing efforts. Interestingly, the order wasn't for a popcorn popper with the New York Jets logo on the side, but for one bearing the Greek letters of the college fraternity Delta Rho Upsilon.

Over the next week, hundreds of orders for poppers bearing the logos for various fraternities poured into his email in-box, bewildering him. How had a blog dedicated to the New York Jets appeared on the radar of some universities that didn't even have football programs?

Upon investigating, he discovered that one fraternity in particular, Delta Rho Upsilon's North Carolina State University chapter, had figured out how to effectively clone his application and reinvent it for their own ends. A trio of students had reverse-engineered the interface to his application, which had been built using Adobe Flash graphics software, and written simple software that passed orders back to Mr. Wunderkind's own blog, thinking he would fulfill them.

Their version never mentioned the New York Jets; it offered popcorn makers printed with any fraternity's Greek letters. "I had not only created a new product inadvertently," Mr. Wunderkind says, "but I had invented a new sales channel."

At that point, he chose to report his findings directly to Ms. Moneymaker, who immediately decided to honor his orders, and to begin selling these customized popcorn poppers in earnest. Ms. Moneymaker, a longtime General Electric executive who rose through the ranks to eventually become chief operating officer of its appliances division, joined Vorpal three years ago to turn around the stagnating division.

"I had had it beaten into me during my time at GE that you had to be #1 or #2 in your industry in terms of market share, or else you should get out. We were #5 when I got here, and no matter how much product we stuffed into our sales channels, we were never going to be #1. This struck me as our chance to pursue a different strategy—to carve out a niche that hadn't previously existed, and to reach a new set of customers who were literally building a new channel for us."

Mr. Wunderkind's efforts initially met a roadblock in the form of Vorpal's chief information officer, Josh Lovecraft, hired by Ms. Moneymaker near the beginning of her tenure. "I was deeply suspicious of Hugo's fraternity brothers at first," Mr. Lovecraft says today. "I just couldn't reconcile exposing our customer database and transaction systems—the heart of this company, in my view—to amateur applications held together with duct tape. The stakes were just too great."

Josh Lovecraft

But faced with pressure from Ms. Moneymaker to shift his own department's resources toward aiding Mr. Wunderkind in his efforts, Mr. Lovecraft hit upon the idea of using web services as the method for linking the efforts of outside innovators such as the North Carolina State students with Vorpal's own systems.

In doing so, he was following the lead of technology companies such as Google and Amazon, which in recent years have invited third party programmers to invent new uses for web applications like Google Earth and Amazon's A9 search engine. The resulting "mashup" applications, as they have come to be known, won acclaim among industry observers, but have not had the bottom line impact that Vorpal's efforts had. "Once we relaxed our guard, we were able to sit back and let our customers bring their orders to us," Ms. Moneymaker says. "Where we had once been so fanatical about controlling our brand image and sales channels, going forward we would make the tools available for our customers to build the channel themselves."

Mr. Wunderkind's toy was quickly rebuilt using services as a full-fledged e-commerce application hosted on Vorpal's web site. But more importantly, the company offered a toolkit to amateur developers so they could build their own applications capable of passing orders back to Vorpal. The company estimates that the toolkit has been downloaded more than 5 million times since being made available in November of last year, and Ms. Moneymaker estimates that approximately 80 percent of Vorpal's custom appliance orders currently originate online, of which only a small fraction arrive via the company's own web site.

The use of services proved to be contagious. In an attempt to automate the laborious process of printing individual decals for each popcorn popper, Vorpal turned to Emblazon Inc. in San Diego, Cal., a decal manufacturer founded by a pair of former competitive surfers that catered largely to the surfing and skateboarding subcultures. Emblazon had already created its own set of web services that effectively transformed its facilities into an on-demand printer. As orders arrived at Vorpal via the mashups scattered across the Web, a second set of services automatically passed the image to Emblazon for printing, setting in motion a process that ended each day with a pallet's worth of decals being FedExed overnight to Vorpal's central manufacturing plant in Malaysia.

"Nothing is more important to our business model than auto-mation," says Emblazon president Michael Herald. "Considering the inherent individuality of each customer's order, we need to do everything in our power to streamline the manufacturing process so as to achieve some economies of scale. We turned to services as a way to receive orders the moment they're posted in our cus-tomers' own systems. We get it when they get it; we bill them and manufacture it, and they never think twice about it."

Encouraged by the early success of Mr. Wunderkind's efforts, and convinced that similar ideas were percolating across the com-pany, Ms. Moneymaker and Mr. Lovecraft quietly polled Vorpal employees on their information technology usage in December of last year. What they discovered, Mr. Lovecraft says, "is that, when it comes to IT, the youngest generation working here has an attitude and a sense of purpose that's distinctly different from our older employees. Rather than practically forcing them to embrace new technologies and then training staff how to use them, they had already turned to a whole new raft of tools like blogs and wikis to help them do their jobs, all under IT's nose."

Mr. Lovecraft dubbed these efforts "Shadow IT," as they were inevitably kept hidden by Vorpal employees from his department. Convinced that another breakthrough similar to Mr. Wunderkind's was possible if they were to nurture these efforts, and concerned that hackers or competitors might exploit them if steps weren't taken to secure these tools, Ms. Moneymaker and Mr. Lovecraft met just before New Year's last year to hammer out a set of policies designed to bring Vorpal's Shadow IT into the light.

Ms. Moneymaker's "New Year's Day" memo, as it became known, was a call to arms on behalf of services. In it, she signaled her willingness to support employees' own projects in much the same way that Google is quick to recognize and supports its engineers' labors of love. But more important was the total commitment to slowly transforming Vorpal's enterprise applications into increasingly large bundles of services.

"My plan all along has been to slowly reinvent this company into one that's leaner, meaner, and more entrepreneurial," Ms. Moneymaker says. "I think our ongoing shift to services is merely the reflection of that in our underlying technology. The real revolution is to change how our employees think about their roles within the company—if they imagine something, we'll provide the technology to support it. That's a big shift from how it's traditionally done, where you force your employees to conform to what the software is capable of."

Earnings in the second half of this year will offer the earliest proof of whether or not Vorpal's strategy will work. While Jabberwocky has already asked other units to convert select applications into services and announced company-wide support for

Shadow IT, it still remains to be seen whether Vorpal can sustain the momentum from its customization efforts over the long term. Exclusive licensing deals with the NFL and MLB have already inspired a range of fan-friendly grilling and other tail-gating equipment, and Mr. Wunderkind hints at a web-driven guerilla marketing effort timed to the World Series next month. As for Vorpal's story so far? "I don't know," he says. "Maybe we'll write a book about it."

The Mechanisms of SOA

While this book strives to tell the story of the business opportunities and cultural changes that are made possible by Service-Oriented Architecture (SOA), we would be remiss if we failed to introduce the underlying concepts and mechanisms that make SOA work.

The definitions and explanations that follow are in no way meant to be the last word on the subject. There are already a great many books on the market explicating the technical details of services at greater length. But without a ground up explanation of SOA, this book would not be complete and would not properly serve readers who are just beginning to understand SOA, or those who have only a general fuzzy idea of the topic. For those who are experts in SOA, the following explanation of SOA will provide an indication of the authors' perspective on the topic.

■ Simplified SOA from Top to Bottom

To properly understand SOA on a level that is relevant to someone who is attempting to make Information and Communication Technology (ICT) work better in a business or other large organization, it is important to understand the context in which SOA was created.

The current architecture of most enterprise applications like ERP, CRM, SCM, and so forth can be boiled down to the oversimplified structure shown in Figure A-1, which this book will refer to as the traditional application stack:

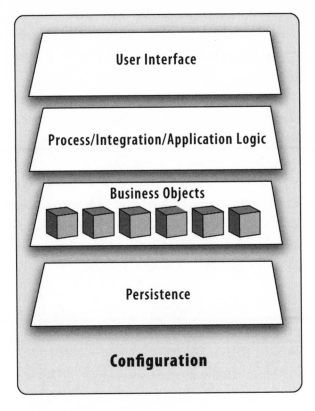

Figure A-1: The Traditional Application Stack

Most applications developed before the year 2000 share this structure, which has the following layers:

- User Interface, which manages communication between people and the application.

- Process/Integration/Application logic, which is the step-by-step instructions set forth in a programming language for transformations of information that do the work of the application.
- Business Objects, which are collections of data and related functionality that are used over and over in an application. One business object might represent customer data; another might take care of product data.
- Persistence, which is another name for the process of storing data in a database or some other permanent fashion.
- Configuration, which is the settings, templates, and other ways of extending the application to adapt to the needs of a particular business.

Figure A-1 is an over simplification because the diagram gives the impression that all of the layers shown are running on the same computer. It doesn't show how client-server architecture separates the user interface onto separate computers or how three-tier architecture separates the application logic and business objects onto even more layers of computers. But these are finer points, the omission of which does not get in the way of our basic message.

Before we get on our high horse about how SOA can do better, we should acknowledge that enterprise applications using this structure run the world. Because SOA can do better, does not mean that all that came before is worthless. Far from it, SOA builds on the past. It does not replace it.

SOA offers the ability to allow standard software to automate many more tasks and processes than is currently the case. The magic of SOA is that it allows this expansion of automation to happen in a way that is flexible and allows changes to occur at a much lower cost than ever before.

To understand how SOA achieves this we must understand how the traditional enterprise applications fit into the context of a large organization. Figure A-2 shows the way that traditional enterprise applications meet many of the requirements for automating the processes of a company.

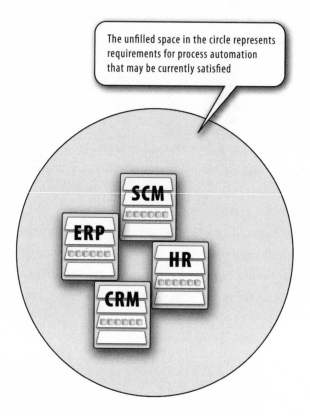

Figure A-2: The Scope of Requirements Met by Enterprise Applications

If we look at Figure A-2 we can imagine that all of the standard software can be extended through configuration to meet the requirements of a business or large organization. The question now is: how does SOA allow standard software to expand the scope or to automate more processes and tasks?

The first concept to understand is the way that SOA breaks up and distributes the traditional application stack into multiple service consumers and service providers that can talk to each other as they wish, as shown in Figure A-3:

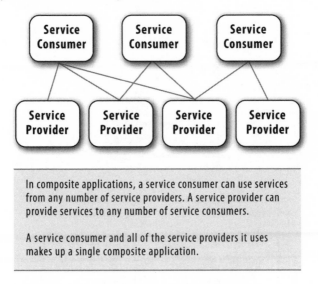

Figure A-3: Multiple Service Consumers and Service Providers

One service consumer can talk to many service providers to get information or to access logic that is needed to do the job at hand. The combination of a service consumer and all the service providers it uses is called a composite application.

How can this possibly work? The answer is that services make it happen. To understand how services work we will return to the traditional application stack and show how it has changed in SOA. Figure

A-4 shows how the parts of the stack have been distributed through-out service consumers and service providers and how services are used to encapsulate business objects and make them reusable.

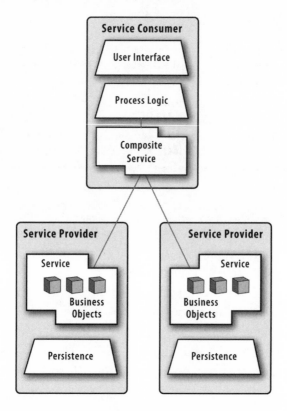

Figure A-4: The Distributed Application Stack in Composite Applications

Figure A-4 shows how the traditional application stack has been broken apart and distributed across service providers using services to allow business objects to be shared. Services provide a way to carve the functionality of an enterprise application or other service provider into reusable chunks that can then be shared across many service consumers to create whatever composite applications are needed. The application and integration logic layers are missing from the picture because those sorts of tasks are now taken care of by services dedicated to performing such jobs.

So far, so good. But there is a trick we haven't mentioned and will discuss in more detail later. Traditional applications are mostly built using what are known as third-generation programming languages that can be used by expert developers to do pretty much anything. Composite applications, of which mashups are one example, are ideally built using model-driven methods which makes development much faster and also allows people to specify applications in a simpler manner. This means that not only expert developers but business people can create composite applications. More potential developers means that more processes can be automated. As we will explain later, something called patterns make model-driven development even more powerful.

One important thing to understand is that SOA doesn't replace traditional enterprise applications, but can actually exist alongside them. Existing enterprise applications often play the role of service providers. So, what will happen with SOA is that the scope of what can be automated with standards software will grow as shown in Figure A-5.

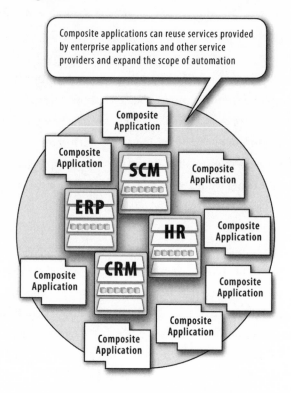

Figure A-5: Using SOA, Composite Applications Expand the Scope of Automation.

So, the effect of SOA is that the range of automation can expand from what is possible in Figure A-2 to what is possible in Figure A-5. And because the expansion will occur by constructing composite applications, which use model-driven development techniques, more people will be able to help in the expansion. Using composite applications, vendors can expand the scope of their products and companies who use those products can extend them further. Changing applications to meet new business needs becomes easier and less costly. Figure A-6 illustrates a before and after comparison of the transformation from the traditional enterprise application stack to SOA.

Traditional Enterprise Applications

An Application is a monolithic conglomeration of business and technical logic ⟷ Within Enterprise Applications many logic functions are duplicated, which makes integration complex and expensive.

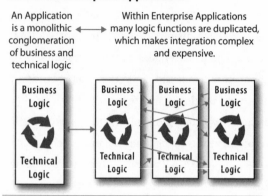

Services in an SOA

Services separate and reuse each element of business and technical logic therefore simplify integration and change

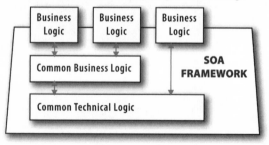

Figure A-6: Enterprise Applications versus SOA.

Taking a step back and looking at the big picture, the impact of SOA can be summarized in the following points:

- SOA allows standard software to meet more business requirements at a lower cost than enterprise applications have been able to do in the past.
- SOA will make development easier by using reusable services as building blocks and model-driven development techniques to put them together.
- Because of SOA, ICT will become responsive to business needs and expand the scope of automation.
- The largest impact of SOA will be the way that expanded automation and flexibility will open the door to transforming business relationships at all levels.

The last point is what this book is all about. Most other books cover the first two points and touch to some extent on the third.

This explanation is sufficient to bring most people up to speed to understand what is going on in this book. But there are a few points that deserve more analysis. The rest of the chapter will cover those.

■ Services

As the name would imply, the fundamental building blocks of SOA are services. A correct, if a bit wonky description of services[1] would be: an "interface to well-defined functionality provided by a service

---

[1] For a comprehensive description of SOA see the Oasis SOA Reference Model, which is located at: http://www.oasis-open.org/committees/tc_home.php?wg_abbrev=soa-rm.

provider." In terms of the explanation just provided, services are usually ways of exposing reusable functionality inside an enterprise application or other service provider so that it can be used to create composite applications or by other service consumers.

For our purposes it might be best to think of services as tiny black boxes of functionality in which requests for functionality go in, and very consciously-defined functionality comes out. They operate on a need-to-know basis. Another service or application sends their requests in the form of messages, and as long as the service replies with the changed data, the application making the request doesn't need to know anything about the internal workings of the service. The human being at the end of this chain of requests doesn't need to know exactly how services work either, and they don't particularly care, which is a major change. All that matters is that well-defined pieces of functionality are used in well-defined ways, and this has major consequences for the next architecture of enterprise applications, as we'll see below.

Service Interface

Services are comprised of at least two layers: the service interface and the service implementation. The visible layer is the interface, which is accessible to all and describes what the service is and how it's used. It is equivalent to the written instructions on the side of our metaphorical black box, explaining what messages can be sent to the service, and what results it is likely to send back.

Service Implementation

The inner workings of the service are shielded from view within the service implementation, which contains the code that summons functionality from the software component the service itself is derived from. The service could be the offspring of an existing enterprise application, or business object, or some special purpose program, or could have been coded from scratch to serve a singular purpose. From a user perspective, it doesn't ultimately matter.

Web Services

It's easy to talk about services in the generic, but in practice—and in the course of this book—we've always been speaking about *web services*. Web services operate in the manner described above, but they are always built around a handful of standards that have already emerged as lingua francas of the SOA world. The service interfaces of web services are described using the Web Services Description Language (WSDL). The data that moves in and out of web services is sent in messages formatted in XML, the eXtensible Markup Language, which is a common language for passing data back-and-forth (usually via the SOAP protocol). Keeping track of web services is made possible by the Universal Description, Discovery and Integration (UDDI) protocol, which is a standard for creating a searchable directory of services for the Service Repository. All of these exist now and are in fairly wide use; they may not be mature technologies yet, but they are having a productive adolescence.

There are major standards efforts underway to add needed elements to the basic web services standards.

Business Objects

Services are not a magic elixir that will make a disorganized application into one that can support services. The key to allowing an existing application to present services to the outside world is the existence of business objects, which are reusable chunks of functionality inside the application that can be used to support services. Many who have tried to make existing applications support services have failed because their applications have a monolithic structure and were not written using properly designed business objects. When services are created on monolithic structures, they tend to be unreliable and have unpredictable side effects. The companies who will win in the race to provide services are those who did a good job of designing their applications in the first place, using reusable business objects.

Composite Services

One of the first required activities when a composite application is created is the design and construction of composite services. Composite services are services created from other services and business objects. Composite services play the crucial role of bringing together all of the information needed by a composite application into one service designed to serve the needs of that composite application. Supporting the creation of composite services is one of the most important duties of composite application development tools.

■ Services Meta Data Repository

One of the major challenges of living in an SOA world is keeping track of what services exist and understanding what each service does.

The main tool provided for keeping track of which services exist is a services meta data repository. A services meta data repository is the master list and ultimate record of every service that exists within the company or organization, and it contains meta data such as WSDL files that describes the properties and proper use for each service. The repository is absolutely vital for keeping track of all the services in use and how, exactly, to use them, so when it comes time to build a new composite service, or composite application, the designers understand what services already exist, and how they interoperate. Think of the repository as the phone book/user's manual for all of your services.

The second challenge is understanding what any individual service does and how it is related to other services. Most vendors who provide services meet this challenge by providing comprehensive models of all of the services they provide that show how each service is connected to each business object and how services work together in the context to automate the processes of a business. These models, which are vitally important to understanding services and sometimes referred to as process component models, may also be kept in the services meta data repository.

■ Composite Applications

Composite applications are the way that SOA delivers value. Without composite applications, all the mechanisms of SOA are merely potentially useful. Composite applications bring everything together and extend the automation to create business value. But composite applications cannot be created in a complicated, difficult to change manner and still deliver on the promise of SOA. The tools to create composite applications must be easy to use and based on model-driven development techniques.

Composition Tools

Composition tools represent a new kind of development environment that uses the services meta data repository as a starting point and allows developers to create composite services and composite applications. The ideal, which is gradually being realized by each successive generation of tools, is an environment in which user interfaces can be constructed and connected to composite services and other services to allow rapid creation of composite applications. In the best case, composition tools will be simple enough to expand the population of developers beyond technical experts to business analysts who are computer savvy enough to use a simplified environment to create composite applications to meet their own needs.

Model-Driven Development

Model-driven development is the way that composite applications will be made flexible and easy to change. Model-driven development replaces complicated coding with a simpler way to express what user interfaces should do, as well as the relationships between services and the business processes that are being automated. Most model-driven development environments for composite applications use a highly visual approach that hides complexity and helps developers through the process. When it comes time to change the applications, models are usually much easier to understand than complicated coding in a third generation programming language. Because modeling hides lots of the details, there is also less chance for errors.

It is important to remember that modeling is a concept that is used over and over again in the world of SOA. As we mentioned in the discussion of the services meta data repository some models are used to explain how services work together. The models used by composition tools are used to construct the behavior of composite applications.

Patterns

In the SOA universe, developing an application again from a blank page will be a rare occurrence. Most often, people will be either configuring a composite application (or service, or whatever) that currently exists, or else they will order up a template that already almost fits the solution requirements. These templates are referred to simply as *patterns*.

The pattern approach recognizes that millions of man-hours have gone into developing applications, and that undeniable best practices have emerged in the course of all that work. In pattern-based modeling, those best practices become another set of building blocks that may not require much customization at all, thus sparing developers the grunt work of connecting services to each other and instead experimenting with optimal combinations instead.

The pattern approach will eventually migrate downward in terms of granularity—picture business objects always built from the same pattern of services (the same ones for searching, for saving, etc.). Building them in this way means that future developers could rest assured that when they wanted to request a service nested within an object from a new application, that service would be utterly predictable in its behavior. That's a vast improvement from trying to tip-toe through the spaghetti code that exists inside of today's enterprise application, and it is precisely those kinds of qualities that will enable SOA to speed up and bulk up your company's supporting IT even as the costs go down.

While this tour of the mechanisms of SOA and related issues has hardly been exhaustive, it should be enough to bring those outside of the world of ICT into the world of SOA so that the rest of the book makes more sense.